THE PLODDY HORSE

THE PLODDY HORSE

An Irish Adventure

Winnie Green

ISBN-13:

Dedicated to Paddy, Pat and Mag (RIP)

Introduction

In 1967 I went on holiday with three college friends .It was an NUS holiday to Ireland , a week in a Horse drawn caravan in Galway . We didn't know what we were letting ourselves in for and as a result there were tears ,laughter ,exhaustion and fun . Most memorable were the experiences involving the horse which are described in this book . All of this happened more than fifty years ago so I am hoping that the owners of any property we damaged are long gone .

Apart from the horse all the characters in this book are fictitious.

Table of Contents

Chapter One - Arrivals

I sat stoically in the rattling plane watching my best friend retching and moaning into the sick bag. It was the first time either of us had flown. Obviously I had the stronger stomach. As Kate leaned back and closed her eyes, I began to wonder if this holiday was such a good idea.

Kate and I, together with Angela and Tricia, had planned this trip months ago. Last September when we started our second year at Teacher Training College we decided that if we had something to look forward to the months would pass more quickly. We searched various National Union of Students (NUS) offers, looking for something different. A week in a horse drawn caravan in green and beautiful County Galway was our exotic choice. The pictures looked great and it seemed an adventurous thing to do, so in January we booked our holiday.

In February my mother died suddenly of a heart attack. She had been suffering for some time with heart disease and although I had noticed she tired more easily, and sometimes could not get her breath, I didn't realise how ill she was. My dad knew and we later found out she had made him promise not to tell us 'kids'. We weren't kids anymore. James is twenty seven, married with a new baby, Sarah twenty five, married last year, Liza twenty three, in her first job as a teacher, and me the baby. All the same, nineteen is far too young to lose your mother. It was a huge shock for me and I was still suffering of course. Kate suggested we cancel the holiday but I really wanted to get away from home and college where I was aware of so much pity and sympathy however kindly meant. The holiday would be a distraction for me, and my older sisters and brother would keep an eye on Dad while I was away. Kate, my best friend, and I had talked about our exotic holiday idea for ages and I knew she would be disappointed if we had to cancel.

In May, Angela had a better offer, a holiday in Greece with her boyfriend and his family. Greece sounded great, her boyfriend wasn't too bad but with his family? Well it was her choice. The remaining three of us decided to leave things as they were, it would mean more space for us and we would split any extra costs between us.

But then, in June Tricia broke her ankle dancing on a common room table while in a drunken state. It was bad for Tricia explaining why she was drunk to Mother O'Brien, who had promptly called her parents to collect the miscreant. It was also bad for the great exotic holiday plan.

After a short discussion about cancelling, short because we would have lost our money, Kate and I decided to advertise in college for two others who were seeking adventure.

For a week there was no response, then just as we were about to accept we would have to cancel, Lizzy and her friend Delia asked to meet with us.

I knew Delia from the Folk Club and we both knew Lizzy by reputation. She was generally accepted as the beauty of our year. Stunning auburn hair and deep blue eyes were her chief attributes, added to that a great figure and a confidence few others in our year possessed. She swept around the college with her group, and Delia was one of them. Apparently however, she missed a lot of lectures, had failed a teaching practice, and was on a final warning . It didn't seem to bother her that much. As far as I was concerned they would both fit in well . As for Kate, she thought Delia was a good fit and the only thing wrong with Lizzy was that she came from London.

Our adventure had begun, Kate travelled down from Hull the previous day and stayed with me last night. We were flying from the new East Midlands Airport.

We were so excited we hardly slept but did manage to be up early for our taxi (my brother). And now, a few hours later, the plane began its descent.

"Cheer up Kate, it looks like we are on our way down," I said.

Kate turned a pale face towards me. "Deo gratias," she whispered.

It didn't take her long to recover once we were on solid ground. Soon we were on the coach to the meeting point at the NUS office in Dublin where Delia and Lizzy, among others, would be picked up. It was our first trip to Dublin and what we could see of it was impressive, especially O'Connell Street and the river Liffey. We couldn't fail to notice we were in Guinness land and as experimenters in the taste of various alcoholic drinks, we looked forward to our first taste of the real stuff.

We remained in our seats near the front of the coach as the newcomers climbed aboard.

"Hi girls," exclaimed Lizzy as she moved towards us, "great to be here, can't wait to for the fun to start."

Lizzy's red hair and blue eyes were shining, she deserved the title of stunner, at 5'5" and slim she was never without male attention. Her friend Delia was perhaps not so glamorous but her curvaceous figure, dark curls and smiley eyes were attractive to many. Both of them had told us they had regular boyfriends.

Kate grimaced at me but said nothing. Then she turned and smiled at Lizzy and Delia, who were now making their way down the coach.

"Did you see that?" she said.

"What?" I replied.

"The ring, how could you miss it?"

"She told us she was engaged, don't you remember?"

"Don't think she is going to act like it," she mumbled.

I looked at Kate.

"Are you jealous of her?" I asked.

"Tess how could you ask that! I may not be a stunner but my blonde hair and brown eyes combination are unusual enough for compliments, and I think my height and athletic figure are an advantage."

"So modest with it," I said laughing.

She smiled at me. "I know, and I am good with kids, which makes me a great teacher."

We both laughed.

To be honest I knew I was the least glamorous of the four of us, however I didn't really care what my mousy brown hair, slim figure and quite adequate facial features looked like. My sadness, which I did my best to hide, was still overwhelming at times.

The coach was now full, excited groups of friends heading out for their Irish holiday.

"Thank goodness they're not sitting near us," said Kate.

"We hardly know them," I said, "give them a chance."

It may seem strange that we didn't see much of each other at college but we were in different education groups and had other social circles. This was definitely a holiday made up of two sets of friends, not the foursome it might look like.

"Well I know from that accent, that we may not get on. You know about Southerners, spoilt and snobby," said Kate.

"Of course only those north of the Wash are tolerable to a Yorkshire lass," I replied smiling, "so how are you going to get on with all these handsome Irishmen we are about to meet ?"

"I'm not looking to meet anyone, remember I have one round my neck already." Kate said.

"And how are things with Pete?" I asked. Kate, unusually, hadn't mentioned him last night.

"Oh I don't know Tess, he wants us to get married and settle down but I am just not sure. I think I love him, but we've been going out for four years now, I haven't really had the chance to look at the other fish in the sea."

"Well let's see what you can hook while we're here," I replied.

I thought I was doing well to distract Kate. We chatted on and I brought her up to date about how my Dad and the rest of the family were coping without Mum. It was easier to talk when sitting beside her and not having to make constant eye contact, I never knew when the tears would come. Kate never fussed over me, like others did, she is such a strong and loving friend, and I can put up with her Yorkshireness. I was just about to tell her this when we were interrupted by Delia.

"Hi just wanted to say how great it is to be here and we are really excited. Lizzy brought these posh biscuits for the journey, hope you like them!" She handed them to Kate then made her way back down the coach.

"Told you," said Kate as she opened the packet. We laughed.

By the time we left the city, the noise on the coach had lessened and we settled down for the trip through central Ireland. It was a distance of 130 miles and would take about three hours with a short comfort stop, the rep informed the coach passengers. Our early morning departure was catching up with us and soon Kate's head was resting on my shoulder. I watched the rather uninteresting scenery while trying not to think about home. I must have dozed off however, as the next thing I knew Kate was gently shaking me. It was good to stretch our legs at the 'comfort' stop which was just outside Athlone.

We spent at least five minutes chatting to Lizzy and Delia before starting on the last part of the journey. The scenery grew more interesting as we travelled westwards and I was delighted to see the sea as we drove through Salthill.

About 5pm we arrived at a farm in Barna on the outskirts of Galway, our Caravan Adventure starting point. As we drove into the yard we saw six caravans lined up. All with a uniform green tarpaulin over the barrelled roof. The stable type doors and outside seats were painted and decorated in different colours

"Just like the photos," exclaimed Kate. All tiredness disappeared as we climbed off the bus and milled around the yard taking a closer look at the caravans.

Altogether there were six groups of four people. A couple of families and the rest were students like us. The man in charge (call me Frank) McKeown, explained what would happen next. First we would be directed to the caravan which would be our home for the next week. We could leave our bags there before we had our evening meal, which was provided. After that we would have an information session covering which farms would welcome us, purchasing essentials, and places worth visiting. We would meet our horses first thing in the morning and be given a lesson on how to shackle up and care for the horse. It was at this point I realised that experience with horses was not one of the subjects we had discussed. I knew Kate and I had very little, basically just seeing them in fields, and we had not asked Delia or Lizzy about their knowledge of horses, if any.

"Here you are girls," called Frank.

"This is your caravan, I'll show you around."

Before showing us inside he walked us round the outside, pointing out the storage cupboard at the back which contained a strong rope, a bag of oats and small spade with a short handle. Kate and I knew what that was for but as Frank said nothing, neither did we. A bucket hung off a hook on the outside of the cupboard. Then he showed us the inside while we stood outside. He pointed out the facilities, it didn't take long.

There were two benches along each side of the caravan. These seats were also our beds, bedding was stored under the seat/bed in a storage box where we put our bags and belongings. There was a counter top with built in sink and a gas ring with two burners. There was one gas light and a torch, two cupboards, one with china and pans and the other for food. Cleaning materials were stored in a corner. There was one drawer with plenty of cutlery, utensils and tea towels. There was a fold down table which was in the front section.

"Put your things away and get yourselves over to the barn now for some supper." Frank advised.

Kate, being the tallest chose her bed first, at the back, I chose the bed opposite. The other two were at the front though to be honest there was little difference, all four of them were very narrow and just short of six feet long.

As he was on his way out Frank looked at us and asked, "Which of you has experience with horses?"

We looked at each other and repeated in turn, "Not me."

Frank shook his head as he called to the next group, four very keen German students, and all men about our age.

We put our things away, exclaiming at the compactness of the caravan and the narrowness of the beds.

"It'll be like sleeping on a church pew," said Delia.

"With a bit of padding," I replied, but feeling just as anxious as the other three looked.

We made our way to the barn.

The shepherd's pie supper served with bread and butter was really tasty and filling. As we drank our tea Kate remarked, "Lizzy, I thought you might know something about horses, didn't you have a pony and do gymkhanas?"

"I don't know where you got that idea from, but no I've never been that interested in riding. Actually I thought you might know something about them, isn't your Dad a farmer?"

"Was - before his accident. We moved to Hull when I was quite little." Kate was abrupt.

"Don't look at me," said Delia, "I like them from a distance, and that's it."

"Maybe we should have thought of this before now. Did you ask us about our experience when we met? I don't remember it coming up in the conversation." said Lizzy.

"That's because it didn't. I never gave it much thought," said Kate.

"Well it's a bit late now, we will just have to get on with it, we're all capable, and how hard can it be?" I added.

"I agree," said Delia, "We'll worry about it tomorrow."

Frank re-appeared and gathered us together for the 'Information session'.

"Here is a map for each van - it shows the main roads and the farms where the farmers are fine with you staying the night on their land. Most of them will sell you milk and eggs, sometimes bread and butter, depends what they have to spare. Try and use these farms, but if you get stuck most places will help you out, just ask. You may have to pay a bit if the farm is not on this list but it won't be much. There are shops in the towns along the way where you can buy food and other things you might need, not like those new supermarkets but good enough."

He went on to talk about places to see - Connemara being the only one I had heard of. It sounded worth visiting. Then it came to questions...

"How far can we travel in a day?" asked one of the German students.

"Depends on the horse," replied Frank, "but the idea is a leisurely holiday. Your horse shouldn't be worked hard every day. Not more than ten miles. That's enough for my horses."

"What about toilets?" asked Kate.

"Good question," said Frank.

I caught sight of Lizzy's face, she looked shocked.

"At the back of the van there is storage for the horses feed and you'll find a small shovel there. If you've been camping you'll know what to do with it and if you haven't, come and see me."

There was some murmuring and even tittering around the room.

Kate, Delia and I knew what he was talking about, but clearly Lizzy did not.

"Don't worry, I'll fill Lizzy in," said Delia, smiling.

There were a few more questions about distances, places to see, and did we need to know how to speak Irish! Then Frank called it a day, suggesting we have an early night ready for an early start. The four of us walked to our temporary home for the week, where Kate and I collected our wash things. We made our way to the washroom and left Delia in the caravan, explaining to Lizzy what life was going to be like for the next week.

When we arrived back Lizzy was sulking, Delia shrugged.

"Look," said Lizzy, "I've told Delia and I'll tell you, there is no way I am going to pee under bushes or shit in a field - just no way!"

"Well if that's how you feel, maybe you better not eat too much for the next few days. This is what we came for isn't it? To be close to real nature not just looking at the pictures," said Kate. I could see she was trying not to smirk.

"I have no problem with being close to nature, I just don't want it sticking up my arse," replied Lizzy, raising her voice. I was trying not to laugh at the picture Lizzy was painting.

"Don't be silly," said Delia, "there will be places we can use a proper toilet: in pubs, cafes and public toilets, of course. Now come on Lizzy, we'll go and use the washroom."

Kate couldn't resist. "Yes it might be the last proper one for a while."

Lizzy gave her a hard look as she and Delia left the caravan.

"That wasn't necessary Kate," I said, "This is the first night of our holiday, can't you please drop your prejudice for a while. There are much worse things than being a Southerner, like dead for example! I'm here to get away from stress and if you don't apologise to Lizzy well..."

I couldn't stop myself from crying .

"Oh God Tess I am so sorry, I can't help putting my big Yorkshire foot in my mouth sometimes. You are right and I'm a twit." She came over and put her arms round me "I am stupid sometimes, I know."

"No, you're not stupid Kate, just Yorkshire. I'm sorry for crying so much, sometimes I wake up in the night with tears rolling down my face, and I just can't control it."

Kate hugged me again.

"You know I'm your friend and always will be Tess, don't worry about the tears. Let's hope the holiday can bring you some happiness, well actually that goes for me too, and I promise I will be nicer to Lizzy."

We got ready for bed and as Lizzy and Delia came in, Kate was retrieving the bottle of duty free vodka and I produced the orange squash.

"Peace offering Lizzy, I was winding you up and I am sorry," said Kate as she poured the drinks and sat down.

"I accept your apology Kate, but I am still worried," said Lizzy.

"I am worried too, but it's more to do with the horse. I'm dreading tomorrow," said Kate.

"Well let's not worry about that until we have to," said Delia.

The rest of the evening was spent discussing the other groups.
"Those kids were a bit cheeky, calling you names Delia," said Lizzy
"Poor things," said Delia, "probably never heard a Scouser before, but I'd rather have them than the serious Germans as travelling companions."
"I don't think we'll be seeing much of them once we start, in fact I think we will be a very long way behind all the other caravans." said Kate.
"Agreed" I said.
We had a few more drinks and played cards for an hour then settled down to sleep. It was only ten pm but I was exhausted. It was all quiet in the yard.
"Good night all, sleep well," I called quietly to the other three. I didn't think I would, but the next thing I heard were the cries of "Guten Morgen." It was seven am.

Chapter Two - Sunday morning

Although it was early, there seemed to be plenty of activity in the yard.

Frank had asked us to be up ‘first thing’ for our instruction session but this was ridiculous, it was only 7 am. When I looked out, it was to see the German students on their way out of the yard with horse and caravan.

“Come on, get up! They’ve already started with the horses,” I said.

There was a lot of muttering and a bit of accidental pushing as we dressed ourselves in the confined space. Somebody suggested only two at a time in the van except when sleeping or eating, a good idea.

We had a quick wash with our damp flannels and then some cereal for breakfast, during which we discussed our approach to the anticipated disaster with the horse.

“We watch carefully and concentrate. Help each other and try not to look too stupid.” said Kate.

“That’s a great idea,” said Lizzy with a note of sarcasm.

Before Kate could respond I chivvied us out and, with coffees in hand, we presented ourselves.

"Good morning girls, it's a beautiful day for you."

Which it was, after yesterday's cloud, but the horse was our pre-occupying thought and we hadn't really noticed the weather.

"Now as it's Sunday and the shops are closed we have a few things over in the barn you might want to buy for your first day on the road," said Frank.

Provisions bought and safely stored, we returned to the yard.

"One group has gone already, Germans are always keen and they know how to handle a horse. I am going to harness up the other groups and I want you to watch."

I breathed a sigh of relief as I realised we would have four groups to study and learn from before it was our turn. The others looked relieved as well.

The only problem was that in all four groups there was least one person who knew a bit about horses. They clearly knew the difference between a head collar and a bridle, had heard of belly straps and traces. The only term I recognized was shafts.

Frank showed each group what to do, and then they had to copy. The horses were obviously used to being harnessed and they stood placidly as the various straps, buckles and bits were applied.

First up were the two families. Although hindered by excited children, both of the Dads paid careful attention. When the group members could harness up without prompts and clues, then they were ready to go. The Dads were brilliant and only needed one practice. The students needed a few more attempts but as they had horse experts in their groups it didn't take them that long. As each group was given the all clear, we waved them off.

As the last group left, my anxiety levels peaked. We were four forlorn figures alone in the yard. Frank had gone to get our horse.

"Why didn't they write all this down and send it to us?" said Delia.

"And would you have read it?" replied Kate.

No-one answered because we knew the answer was 'No'.

"I'll never remember all that stuff," I said.

"You don't have to remember all of it as long as we can do it all between us," Lizzy replied.

"Lizzy is right, just let's look as if we know what he is talking about and when we have to actually practice, help each other," said Kate.

"Where's our horse anyway?" The words were hardly out of Delia's mouth when we heard the clip clop behind us.

"Bloody hell – that horse is huge!" Kate exclaimed, and we all stared at the beast. We were speechless, I for one was in agreement with Kate. We looked at each other, there was definitely an air of panic.

"Now don't panic girls, this old mare is a great horse, gentle as you could ever find. Yes she's big but you're four strong lasses, you can handle her."

"What's her name?" I asked.

"You can call her whatever you like, I call her Daisy, because she is so white."

"Does she have yellow eyes?" Lizzy muttered.

"Now come on and say hello to her."

We walked over and patted her neck gingerly.

"I can't see over her back," said Delia, "she's much bigger than the others."

"Now girls she's only a bit bigger and you were never close enough to the others to judge their size. You'll be fine girls – she's a great beast, I promise youse. Now I hope you have been paying attention to the other groups, it's time to harness up."

All the items needed were in the back of a wagon which he pulled over in front of 'Daisy'.

"You don't have to remember the names of everything but you do need to know the order of things. We'll start with the bridle, pull her head down by holding onto the halter and just slip the bridle over her head getting the bit into her mouth. Now who is going to do this?"

We all looked at Kate.

"You're the tallest and the strongest," I said by way of explanation.

"Ok, I'll do it this time but we should all have a go sometime."

"Agreed," we said in unison and with a slight sense of relief.

Frank demonstrated the placing and order for the bridle, collar, hames, straddle, reins, belly strap and back band, traces, breeching strap, and tug strap. We watched attentively. At each step Kate had to repeat what he had demonstrated then go onto the next. There were ten different steps. We applauded Kate when she had completed the task. I knew, as I am sure the others did, that Frank was a useless teacher for beginners like us. And so it proved. He removed all the harness, except the bridle and invited Kate to 'harness up'.

"I've done the first one for you - so carry on now..."

Kate put on the collar, looked at us, then Frank. We all nodded encouragingly. Then she put on the straddle, we nodded encouragingly again but Frank shook his head. It went downhill from then, as Frank realised he was dealing with four incompetent dreamers. However he didn't give up and neither did we. After an hour and a half he accepted that in our case it would be a group effort for harnessing and un-harnessing Daisy. Eventually we passed the test and were allowed to leave the yard, once we had listened to the lecture. It covered feeding the horse, places to stay, and a few general rules – keep left when driving, always have someone walking with the horse. Ask the farmer before you enter his property, no driving after dark.

"Now decide who's doing what and you can be on your way." Clearly he was as relieved as we were at our departure.

"I think I should be first driver since I suffered the most humiliation," said Kate.

"You weren't the only one Kate, I don't think any of us came out of it covered in glory, or found we had hidden horse management skills," said Delia. "I'll walk with the horse first, until we stop for lunch."

Lizzy and I took up our places on the seats either side of the door, Kate now stood behind the half open door with the reins in her hands. She flicked the reins as Delia pulled Daisy gently at the front end.

"Gee up Daisy!"

Daisy plodded her way out of the yard, probably thinking she had suffered most of all in the last few hours.

We were well clear of the yard and Kate shouted,

"Three cheers for us, we're here - Hip Hip Hooray!!"

We all joined in - it marked the release from the last hours of anxiety and the proper beginning of our holiday.

Daisy continued to plod, both Kate and Lizzy shook the reins and called "Gee up" but Daisy was deaf to their calls. The three of us in the van discussed the technical feat we had accomplished and then the subject changed to distance, time and food, basically how far was it to the nearest stopping place, how long would it take us to get there and what would we have to eat. These three topics would become major talking points in the next week. At the moment we had no answers so we were forced to carry on in ignorance. Delia assured us she was quite happy walking alongside Daisy even though the road was very quiet. I was just happy swinging my feet and enjoying the countryside. To our right green meadows with cows, and a few sheep, to our left what looked like heathland barren and dark. This would be the Moycullen bogs which were on the map Frank had supplied. None of us had seen a peat bog before so when we came to a crossroads I suggested we took a left turn so that we could explore further. All agreed, and we had only travelled a few hundred yards when we met a man coming the other way.

"And where might you be going girls?"

"To see the bog," replied Delia.

"Wherever the road takes us," Lizzy smiled.

"Sure if you go much further you'll be in the bog. Didn't you notice the road was narrowing ?" he asked.

We had to admit we hadn't.

"You'll have to turn round here where you just might make it. I'll lead the horse, the four of you make sure the wheels stay on the road."

We were not too happy about this but obviously he knew more than we did so we jumped down out of the caravan and waited for further instructions.

"Watch the back wheels," said our new friend as he took control of Daisy and began to turn her.

On either side of the road was a drop into the bog. It was beginning to look a bit scary.

Suddenly Lizzy who was on the far corner shouted, "Shit! The wheel's going down into the ditch!"

"Put your backs into it then," came the swift reply.

The four of us pushed and shoved as much as we could and slowly the van came upright and our saviour completed the turn. He handed the reins to Kate.

"Off you go now girls and take my advice - stick to the main road in future, unless you know where you are going." And he marched off with a broad smile.

We went back to our positions feeling chastened.

"I think we should take a break soon, I could really do with a coffee after that experience," said Kate.

"Ok, Lizzy, why don't we go on ahead and see if there is a good place to stop," I said.

Lizzy and I walked on, sharing our feelings about what had just happened and agreed it was an adventure to remember and that we were not as clever as we thought we were. Before long we found an excellent lay-by with a wide green verge where Daisy could have some lunch too. The lay-by was bordered by a dry stone wall and there was even a bin.

Kate and Delia guided Daisy very proficiently and stopped. Frank had told us if we stopped for a very short time it was okay to keep Daisy harnessed but if we were stopping for a while, then we should un-harness her. We agreed we would be at least an hour so Kate and I set about getting Daisy out of the shafts and un-harnessed.

"I'll get on with the sandwiches and coffee," said Lizzy.

"I'll do the washing up," added Delia.

We put the harness down carefully as Frank had told us. Kate and I congratulated ourselves, bathed in the glow of success as we tethered Daisy to a very large stone on the dry wall behind the caravan. We joined the others for lunch.

"Great sandwiches Lizzy," I commented.

"I'm glad you like them, cheese and pickle with salad, one of the best I make. I am good at sandwiches, even if I say so myself. It makes up for the fact that I can't cook," replied Lizzy

"What do you mean, you can't cook or you don't cook?" said Kate. I could see her hackles rising.

"Same difference," said Lizzy.

Before anyone could respond there was a great clattering noise outside at the back of the caravan.

"Oh my God, what's happening?" I thought as we pushed and shoved our way outside.

Daisy was on the other side of the road, reins trailing behind her still wrapped round the large stone. She was oblivious to us or to the section of wall she had pulled down.

Kate showed her mettle.

"Tess, you retrieve the bloody horse, Lizzy you and I will start putting the wall together and Delia you go and clear the lunch things so we can get away as soon as we harness up."

We sprang into action. I managed to retrieve the bloody horse by pulling on her head collar and telling her off for thinking the grass was greener on the other side - it wasn't.

Kate and Lizzy were doing their best to rebuild the wall but it was not going well. Delia was the first to finish her allotted task. The lunch things cleared, she appeared from the caravan.

"I'll help Lizzy with the wall while you and Tess harness the horse. You're the one with the most experience Kate," said Delia. Her attempt at humour went unnoticed as Kate muttered her agreement.

"Get the bridle Tess, I know that's first," said Kate "now I just need to get her head down and then..."

But Daisy was not co-operating, every time Kate managed to get her head down far enough to place the bridle, she raised and tossed her way out of Kate's grip

"Come on you bloody horse," Kate almost shouted.

"We need to get out of here, can't one of you help?" she said looking round.

Lizzy and Delia were still deciding which stone went where and the discussion was beginning to be less than amicable.

I went round to the other side of the horse and we both tried to pull her head down but as soon as Kate loosened her grip to place the bridle and bit, we were shaken off.

"Open your mouth you damned horse, we gave you a good lunch break now come on!!!"

But it was to no avail. Kate looked at me.

"Any ideas?" she said.

"Well I remember when I was in the guides someone saying you can make any animal open its mouth if you stick your fingers up its nostrils."

"You're kidding," said Kate.

"Have you got a better idea?"

"Bugger it, we'll give it a try, you get on my shoulders."

"You mean I have to stick my fingers up its nose?"

"Well it was your idea."

"Why do I have to get on your shoulders?"

"We can pull her head down, you will able to reach her nostrils and I can slide the bit into her mouth when she opens it."

"Kate, I'm really not sure about this, I don't even know if it's true..."

"Shut up and get on my shoulders."

There had been many occasions in the past when I had sat on Kate's shoulders. When getting over the college wall after hours, or performing in a PE display but never anything involving any sort of animal. I was not happy.

Kate bent down and I reluctantly climbed onto her shoulders, she stood up gripping my feet as I waved two fingers of my left hand towards Daisy's nostrils. Thankfully Lizzy and Delia were engrossed in their quarrelling about which stone should go where so no-one could witness my humiliating act.

But then from behind us came a masculine voice - obviously choking back laughter.

"Haway girls what do you think you're doing - poking out a horse's eyes?"

Kate turned round quickly, I almost fell off.

"This bloody horse won't let us put the bit in its mouth so Tess is trying to make it open its mouth," she said in a rush, blushing madly.

"How - by poking its eyes out?"

"Of course not," replied Kate, "Tess is going to put her fingers up its nostrils."

There were shouts of laughter from him as well as Lizzy and Delia.

I was trying to keep my cool but clearly we had been caught in a very stupid act. Kate let me down and we stood more embarrassed than we had ever been in a joint venture.

"Give me the bridle," he said when he eventually stopped laughing.

He, of course, put it on expertly then helped us with the rest of the harness.

"My name is Dermott, happy to oblige, your man should've told you when you take out the bit the horse thinks its work is finished for the day, and, by the way you never tether a horse with the reins, there will be a rope somewhere in the van for tethering but I guess youse have learned a lesson." He was still smiling. "And if you get as far as Galway, go to Ryans bar. I'll buy youse all a drink for giving us all a great laugh."

He winked very deliberately at Kate then walked towards his car. There was a great cheering and at least three lads waved at us with big grins on their faces.

I felt mortification upon mortification.

"Let's get out of here," said Kate quietly.

I knew she felt as bad as I did.

Chapter Three -Sunday afternoon

"Who would like to be the driver now?" asked Kate.

"Yes please," said Lizzy "I just hope I am better at driving a horse than driving a car, I failed my test last week."

Kate said nothing but gratefully handed over the reins.

'I'll walk with Daisy then," I said. Truthfully, I wanted to be on my own for a while, still smarting from my recent humiliation.

"Are you sure Tess, you look a bit miserable," said Kate.

"Well I feel a bit miserable Kate, Daisy will be excellent company for me right now."

I turned and took hold of the head collar, leading us back on to the road. Lizzy was making clicking noises and shaking the reins, Daisy remained as responsive as ever and plodded on. I knew Kate would be upset by my remark but frankly I didn't care and I said as much to the horse.

It didn't take me long to realise that Daisy was a great listener, I could say whatever I liked and she never answered back. I started telling her how I thought I had made a big mistake by even coming on this holiday. I missed my Mum and I knew my Dad was struggling, although there were other family members to look after him, I was the last one at home. Undistracted by any traffic I was soon crying again. I was comforted by Daisy's various snorting noises and the warmth coming from her neck. I was only slightly conscious of the laughter and conversation behind me, feeling more at peace with the horse than with the other three. After the day we'd been having I should have known it wouldn't last. We were passing a small cottage when a distraught woman came running to the gate.

"Maisie, oh Maisie, what have they done to you?" She hurried round to me and without more ado pulled down the head collar and stroked Daisy's nose.

"That old bugger, he promised me Maisie would be retired and not to have to work any more. Look at you, she's pulling a caravan and four galumphing girls, it's not right, it isn't." She began to cry and I couldn't think of anything to say. Daisy/Maisie was not showing any sign of recognizing her previous owner, she just breathed rather noisily.

Lizzy from behind the door stepped up.

"This horse is called Daisy, so we were told, but we can call her Maisie if it would make you feel better," said Lizzy. "If you have any concerns about her you need to speak to Mr. McKeown at Barna. Now we have paid for this holiday, so please step back and we'll be on our way." She flicked the reins and I pulled the horse on. The woman stepped back, dabbing at her eyes with her apron.

"It seems I'm not the only one with problems," I said to Daisy/Maisie with a smile. Kate joined me.

"Are you feeling any better?"

I realised I did.

"Yes, a bit I suppose."

"Delia says she'll walk the horse again while you and I go on and find the farm we are staying at tonight."

"Do you think Lizzy will be okay with the horse?" I asked, surprised at Kate's trust in her.

"I don't think she'll be either worse or better than the rest of us," Kate replied, "I'll be glad to get away from the horse for a while, she's brought us enough trouble for one day."

"I don't think we can blame her for everything that's gone wrong, especially that last one, the woman seemed a bit doolaly, don't you think?"

"Maybe there are a lot of big white mares in this area," said Kate.

For some unknown reason I found this funny. Delia appeared so I handed over to her while Kate and I walked on to find Clarkins Farm, the first one on Frank's list.

"What was all the laughing about earlier on," I asked.

"What do you think?" said Kate, "It was about one of the most embarrassing and humiliating moments of my life, and yours, I suspect. Lizzy and Delia just couldn't stop laughing. They asked what we were thinking of, tying the horse to a big stone when it had just been drawing a caravan with three of us in it, as if the stone would stop the bloody horse from wandering."

"They have a point," I said.

"I know they do, but it doesn't help the situation knowing we were stupid. We must have looked really ridiculous and I'm just not ready to laugh about it yet."

"Me neither," I said, and after a short silence, "How far is it to this farm?"

"About ten minutes walk I would say."

Twenty minutes later we arrived at Clarkins Farm. I was a bit anxious about the barking dogs in the yard but Kate ignored them. Before we reached the door it was opened. Mr Clarkin (call me Pat) knew Frank and was very welcoming.

"Just pull in the gate and wait for me there, I'll keep an eye out for yous. I'll show you where the paddock is for the horse. Now would you like some eggs and milk?"

We negotiated a price, thanked him and walked back to find the van.

"That damned horse," said Kate, "I can't forgive her for being so stubborn with us, making us look like right idiots."

"It's not her fault if we can't manage her," I replied.

"You're being much too nice Tess, would you still think so if you had put your fingers up her nose?"

"I'll put my fingers up your bloody nose in a minute," I said.

"But I haven't got a bloody nose."

"Do you want one?" I said, giving her a fake punch as we fooled around laughing.

By the time we reached the caravan we were both feeling more cheerful about things.

"Did you ask about the toilet?" asked Delia.

I confessed we hadn't but I would ask when we arrived at the farm.

Mr Clarkin (call me Pat) was true to his word. Shortly after our arrival he walked down to the caravan with the eggs and milk and began to help with the horse.

"Is this your first day girls? I hope you've had a good one. Some interesting sites between here and Barna eh."

I had the overwhelming feeling he knew about our shaming episode, so I distracted him by asking:
"Do you know where we could find a bathroom?" hoping he would offer the use of the farmhouse.
"Aye, Reilly's Hotel down the road in Moycullen, I think there's a sink in the ladies too, they'll be open now for a couple of hours, won't take you long to walk there."
It was about 5 pm and a beautiful evening so after feeding the horse and taking her to the paddock we went for a walk to find a bar with a toilet, or even a toilet without a bar, which for me would have been preferable.
Reilly's bar had about four customers so we doubled business when we arrived.
There was an awkward silence which eased slightly when we ordered four pints of Guinness.
"Oh, not for me," said Delia, "I think it's a bit strong. I'll have lemonade."
There was a bit of banter about 'young ladies out drinking on their own', but we told them we were holidaying in a travelling caravan.
"Like tinkers," said Lizzy and the four drinkers turned away from us, unsurprisingly. We took ourselves to a table as far as possible from the bar.
"For goodness sake Lizzy, don't you realise how insulting that remark is," said Kate.
"Well no, not really, should I apologize do you think?" said Lizzy.
Kate rolled her eyes. "I'm going to the Ladies," she said.

I explained to Lizzy that she should not apologise and we would talk later about some rules of etiquette while we are in Ireland. Then I changed the subject before Kate arrived back.

"What are we having for tea?" I said.

"Well we bought eggs, bread, cheese and some salad stuff this morning," said Delia as she rose to go to the Ladies.

"And we had more eggs and bread from Pat," said Lizzy.

There was a short discussion about the possibilities.

"French toast," I suggested.

"Boiled egg salad," suggested Lizzy.

"Seems to me that omelettes would be a good idea," said Kate. "I'll show you how to make one Lizzy. In fact you could even have a go at making your own."

I knew that Kate was taunting Lizzy, and was relieved to see Delia return to her seat.

"Well, have you made a decision?" she asked.

"Kate has suggested omelettes, and I think she has offered to make them all," I said.

"Not quite all," Kate said, giving me a withering look which I ignored. I turned to Lizzy.

"Why don't you go next to the toilet Lizzy, then I'll go last."

"That's fine, I will, thanks Tess," said Lizzy.

Kate gave me another one of her looks, I had spoiled her fun.

"Are you alright Delia?" I said, "You seem a bit quiet, I thought you would have been rolling out the songs today."

We knew Delia had a wonderful voice - sweet, yet strong and pitch perfect. She was a regular at the folk club and often sang Irish folk and rebel songs.

"No, not today, I am still recovering from the journey yesterday," she said, "hopefully I'll feel up to it soon," and she swigged her lemonade.

We were not feeling very welcome in the bar so as soon as I had finished at the bathroom we gulped down our drinks and left.

"So there was a sink in there," said Delia "we should bring our wash things when we go to the pub in future."

"Good idea," replied Lizzy.

We walked home in our pairs, chattering friends.

As we reached the caravan Kate reminded Lizzy about the cooking plan.

"If you show me how it's done I will have a go," said Lizzy "But let's eat outside, it's such a beautiful evening." We agreed.

"I'm starving so I'll get on now with the omelettes," said Kate "if you three could get on with the salad and grate some cheese. The salad needs to be ready with bread and butter before I start cooking."

Delia and I cut the bread and washed the salad, Lizzy grated the cheese. Then we watched Kate cook a perfect cheese omelette which she handed to Delia. Mine was next then her own, both just as perfect as the first.

"Are you ready Lizzy? Here are your eggs and some cheese let's see how you get on," said Kate.

Considering she had an audience Lizzy did well, although not up to Kate's standard of course.

"Not bad at all," said Kate, and she actually smiled at Lizzy who smiled back.

I felt such relief, the atmosphere between the two of them was beginning to mellow. I went inside to make the tea. Five minutes later I came out with the mugs and the mellowing had stopped. Lizzy barged past me into the caravan, Delia was sitting on her own, no sign of Kate.

"What happened?" I asked.

"Oh you know what those two are like, Lizzy asked Kate what was wrong with calling ourselves tinkers! Kate gave her a filthy look and walked off."

Just then Lizzy re-appeared,

"I'm going to see the horse," she said. She had collected her drawing materials from the caravan, and was now marching off towards the paddock.

"Why doesn't she understand?" I asked.

"Lizzy is not like us," said Delia. "I guess you and Kate are like me and we learned a version of Irish history at our grannies' knee, it's bred in us but not Lizzy. For a start she comes from a privileged English family, her father is some kind of business man who travels the world and her mother often goes with him."

"Definitely not like my background," I said.

"Nor mine, but she is not as lucky as us in many ways."

"Such as?"

"Such as, Lizzy wanted to go to Art school but her parents wouldn't hear of it. They said she had to do teacher training as then she would have a means of supporting herself. If she wanted to do something else when she qualified, then it would be up to her."

"That sounds sort of reasonable," I said.

" The trouble is Lizzy hates college, she will be the first to admit that teaching is not for her, and I wouldn't be surprised if she fails her final teaching practice and exams," said Delia.

"But if her parents have plenty of money, then it just seems mean to force Lizzy into something she doesn't want to do," I said.

"Well they're mean all right - they have too much money for Lizzy to qualify for a grant. She is completely dependent on them financially, and they are not exactly generous. In fact Lizzy has much less than we have for spending money, and they have an arrangement with the college to keep an eye on her. I wouldn't be surprised if they paid the nuns to do it."

"What are you two being so serious about?" said Kate who had crept up behind us.

"I'll tell you later," I began.

"Oh we were just talking about what kind of tinkering we should do tomorrow - pots and pans or what."

It was the first time I had heard Delia crack a joke and it was a good one. The three of us laughed.

We could see Lizzy on her way back, sketch in hand.

"I think I'll get the vodka out, it's been a long day," said Kate.

It was beginning to get dark but not too dark to admire Lizzy's drawings of Daisy. They were exceptional to my eye.

"Wow, they are brilliant Lizzy," I said, knowing Kate's curiosity would bring her out to look.

"Yes I guess they are pretty good," said Kate albeit grudgingly.

"I'm quite pleased with them myself, even though the light was not so good. Maybe this holiday won't be so bad after all, if I can get more sketching in."

"What do you mean, 'won't be so bad after all'?" said Kate.

Lizzy gave her a long look.

"Forget it, it's been a long day and I'm tired, pass the vodka Delia."

“One vodka and orange for me please, what about you Kate?” I said making sure Kate could see my best ‘Shut up or else’ glare.

The sun had gone down and there was a slight chill in the air so we went inside. The next hour or so was spent in relatively peaceful activity. I enjoyed lighting the gas lights recalling my childhood holidays in caravans by the sea, the gas popped when it lit and I could hear my Mum's voice reminding my dad to be careful with the mantle, they were so fragile they would break if you touched them too heavily with the lighted match. I tried not to dwell on the picture of my Mum, letting it pass gave me the feeling of a pleasant memory.

Lizzy was working on the sketches of the horse and Kate was writing up her diary.

"Have you written to Pete yet?" I asked.

"Nothing to write about really, I’ll probably send him a postcard when I buy one."

"What do you mean nothing to write about!" said Delia. "We nearly landed in a bog, the horse pulled a wall down, we were practically attacked by a mad woman and we learned how to harness a horse, all in one day."

"Not to mention making a complete fool of yourself in front of a very handsome Irishman," I added.

Whether she wanted to admit it or not I could see that Pete was on his way out as far as Kate was concerned.

Kate smiled: "I'll send him a postcard soon," she said, and carried on with her diary.

"Well I think we’ve had an exciting day," I said and settled down with my book.

"I would like a few exciting nights," said Lizzy without lifting her eyes from her drawing.
"Agreed," said Delia and Kate
"Last one awake turns out the light." I said.

Chapter Four- Monday

Monday morning, and we all woke early to another beautiful day. Last night's tetchiness forgotten, we sorted breakfast and ate on the steps of the caravan enjoying the sun on our faces. Kate disappeared inside then re-appeared with the information sheet provided by Mr. McKeown.

"Well, after yesterday what do you think we should do today?" Kate asked.

I think she felt the need to organise things if we were to avoid any more calamities.

We sat around the table and looked at the map supplied, although Lizzy did not seem that interested.

"Shall we try and get to Oughterard? It's a bit further than we managed yesterday but we'll have an earlier start," suggested Kate.

And hopefully not as many setbacks, I thought.

"Well, I would like to have a proper wash, and wash my hair," said Lizzy.

Kate looked at her for a second and then replied, "Okay I guess we could all do with a bath, but we are not likely to find one round here. Let's get going and see what we can find." There was an edge to her voice which I could hear but I didn't know if the other two picked it up.

There was a shout from outside, it was Mr. (call me Pat) Clarkin.

"Thought you'd be up girls – it's a great day for yous. Do you need a hand with harnessing up?"

"Yes please," smiled Lizzy.

And Kate spoke at the same time, "No we'll be fine, thanks all the same..."

The farmer looked from one to the other.

"Could you just watch us to make sure we do it right?" I said giving Kate a glare.

Kate responded by transferring her annoyance into energy and she confidently put on the bridle, shocking herself at Daisy's acquiescence in letting the bit pass over her teeth.

Lizzy disappeared inside the caravan and the three of us finished harnessing up supervised by the farmer.

"That's grand girls, you did a fine job, have a good day now. Where are you off to?"

"Oughterard, how far do you think it is?" asked Kate.

"Och about 10 miles – easy in a day."

Lizzy came back. "Do you know somewhere we could get a wash?" she asked.

She looked at Kate, who turned away from her.

"Well there's a good stream down the road a mile or two and a spring, nice soft water," said the farmer. Lizzy was speechless, Kate noticed.

"Thanks very much for all your help," said Kate as she stepped up into the caravan. Mr. Clarkin smiled broadly then went about his business.

"Lizzy you're so keen for your wash, why don't you walk out in front with the horse and see if you can find this stream."

Kate was fighting to keep the sarcasm from her voice. Before Lizzy could reply I interrupted.

"Kate, could I stay with Daisy today? I really like walking with her."

Kate looked at me.

"Are you sure, you walked all day yesterday...?"

"I'm sure," I said ,then went and stood by the horse waiting for the others.

"Is she all right?" I heard Lizzy ask Kate.

I left them to speculate and gave Daisy an affectionate rub on her neck.

Delia called, "Gee up," and I led us on to the road.

I could hear Lizzy muttering :

"Washing in a bloody stream for God's sake, what other indignities are we going to have to suffer?" Both Delia and Kate responded but I couldn't hear what they said. About a mile down the road I heard laughter from Lizzy and Delia although not Kate. I found out later the cause was Kate's insistence they cleaned the horse's bum every time she dropped a load of manure. It had led to her being called the loo roll monitor and "she just couldn't see the funny side," reported Delia to me later.

Unaware of the controversy at the time I continued my whispered conversation with Daisy.

"I really shouldn't have come on this holiday, I realise that now, and God knows why I feel so loyal to Kate... No, that's not true. I don't know what I would have done without her these last few months when I couldn't talk to anyone else. All the rest of the family are so bound up in grief and being at home is like walking on eggshells. Kate was there just for me."

The horse neighed gently.

"You're such a good listener Daisy, I could talk to you all day long."

We walked on for about half an hour, when there was a shout from Delia.

"Wow he was right, look at that!"

As we came round a bend there was a wide verge with a stream flowing alongside.

I led Daisy on to the verge. It was perfect, the stream was screened from the road by bushes, at the far end there was a lay by and the spring water well the farmer had mentioned.

The sun was shining strongly, it was an ideal time and place for a wash. Clearly we would be here for an hour at least so Delia and I freed Daisy from the shafts, remembering the lessons from yesterday. We found a rope in the storage box and tethered her to the back of the caravan. This time we did not remove the bit and bridle. We gathered our wash things and each found ourselves a spot on the bank of the stream well hidden by bushes from the eyes of any passing motorists. Lizzy was not happy.

"There is no way I am washing in there," said Lizzy, "there could be a dead anything further up stream. I'll go and wash my hair in the spring."

"Please yourself," said Kate.

The rest of us stripped off, although as good Catholic girls we maintained some decency. The water was very pleasant, cool and refreshing. Above our splashings we could hear Lizzy yelling about the coldness of the spring water. Kate instructed us when it came to cleaning our teeth, the person furthest upstream went last. We then took turns at hair washing and found Lizzy was right, the water was so cold it made my head ache.

Lizzy gave in.

"Well I guess I shouldn't be the only smelly one," she said as she took herself upstream for a wash.

It was such a perfect spot we decided to stay and have an early lunch. Kate and I made the sandwiches while Lizzy and Delia sat outside near the well drying their hair, bare legged and bare footed.

A large car came slowly towards us and stopped about fifty yards away. We watched as the doors opened and four colourfully clad people, two men and two women, emerged. The two men had fancy cameras. Americans, I guessed correctly. They addressed Delia and Lizzy:

"Gee are you real tinkers... Can we take your photo?"

Delia and Lizzy looked at each other, Kate and I looked at each other.

"Aye, youse can look and take your picture but it'll cost you a dollar," said Delia in a very approximate version of a West Coast Irish accent.

"Sure." They handed over the dollar. "Can we look inside?"

Kate and I, trying to stifle our laughter, suddenly stopped.

"No, no the caravan is sacred to us and it would bring youse bad luck if you went in there, unless you were invited by Mama, and she's asleep," explained Delia.

"OK, gee but we are so lucky to come across you, like this," gushed one of the women. Kate pretended to snore loudly, and I had to stuff my towel to my mouth to stop myself laughing aloud. We could hear them walking round the caravan clicking away. I came out to join Lizzy and Delia, assuring them in my best Irish accent that Mama was still asleep. The visitors took a couple more pictures, handed over a few more dollars and drove on. Over lunch we re-played the scene and practiced the Irish accent. It was a good laugh.

"I do drama at college," said Delia, "but don't think I've done that accent before."

"That's because you just made it up," said Lizzy, laughing."And Americans really do say gee. We should have taken a photo of them."

It prompted her and Kate to find their cameras. They took some silly shots and other picturesque views including Daisy.

I realised this was the first time we had all been happy together, maybe things were looking up. I really hoped so.

I went to start harnessing Daisy but she refused to move, and she wasn't grazing.

"Come on bloody horse what's wrong with you?" I pulled hard on the head collar then noticed she was holding her front left hoof off the ground.

"Kate, you better come here, there's something wrong with Daisy," I said.

"Knew it was too good to last," I heard Kate mumble as she approached.

"There's something wrong with her foot," I said.

"Let's have a look, I saw on Blue Peter how to lift a horse's foot ready for shoeing," she said.

Kate turned her back to us and grabbed the long hair around the mare's foot and lifted the hoof. Surprisingly Daisy co-operated fully.

"There's the problem, a nail in the soft part of the foot, it's come from the shoe," she said.

We gathered to inspect it.

"Don't suppose we have one of those things for taking the nails out of horse's hooves," I said.

"Maybe not, but I know something which might work," Kate said.

She went into the caravan, and re-appeared shortly with a dinner fork.

"You hold her foot up Tess, while I get the nail out," she said.

We watched with admiration as Kate slid the nail between the tines on the fork and began to pull. The nail was soon removed and Daisy snorted her thanks.

"Good old Blue Peter," said Kate.

However we still had a problem as Daisy now had a loose shoe and all four of us could see it needed attention.

"Lizzy, could you and Delia go ahead and try to find out if there is a blacksmith near here?" said Kate, and they set off without question or comment.

"Well that's a bit better," I said.

"What do you mean?" replied Kate.

"You asked rather than ordered."

Kate and I carried on with the tidying up and preparing to leave.

"You know I'm really trying Tess, I don't know why, but southerners like Lizzy always rub me up the wrong way. I haven't anything against her, I hardly know her for goodness sake but as soon as she opens her mouth..."

"And as soon as you open yours you show your prejudice. Come on Kate, I know what a really patient and kind person you are. Just listen to what Lizzy is saying and ignore the way she's saying it, if you can .You obviously don't feel the same about Delia."

"Yes but she's from Liverpool, not London," said Kate, then after a pause added, "Delia seems very quiet, is she normally like this?"

"Actually no, I've been out with her group a few times, she's usually lively and very funny," I said, "you saw how she acted today with the Americans, that's typical Delia."

"Your acting was quite good too, and you enjoyed it!" said Kate

"Well it does seem a long time since I have found anything really funny, it still feels a bit not right to laugh, not that it's wrong of course..."

I was lost for words. This happened all the time when Mum first died, I would be in the middle of a sentence then lose the thread of what I was saying. In the last few weeks it seemed to be happening less.

"Sorry Tess, I keep forgetting," said Kate you know I have never experienced the grief you are feeling, but I do know it won't last for ever and your Mum would definitely want you to laugh, she always enjoyed a joke. I bet she would have laughed at our goings on yesterday."

"Yes, she would have laughed her head off," I said shedding silent tears.

We sat quietly watching Lizzy and Delia making their way back.

"There's a Smithy about a mile down the road," said Delia, "and the chap we spoke to thinks it will be okay for Daisy to pull the caravan there. We just have to watch that she doesn't lose the shoe."

"All right," said Kate, "I guess we should get moving."

Daisy seemed more amenable than usual while we put her back into the shafts.

"I'll walk with you Tess, on the other side of the horse, in case we have to stop again," said Lizzy.

"Good idea," I replied.

Kate took up the reins and offered them to Delia.

"No thanks," she said "if it's okay with you I'd like to read for a bit," and disappeared inside.

Kate shrugged. I took my place and led Daisy on to the road.

"Have I done something to upset Kate?" asked Lizzy. This was probably the first time we'd had a chance to speak, just the two of us.

"No, it's nothing you've done, more something that you are."

"What do you mean?"

"You're a Southerner, a Londoner," I hesitated then added, "and posh."

To my surprise Lizzy laughed.

"Well I can't deny I am a Londoner, but what's wrong with that?"

"Nothing at all, unless you're like Kate and dyed in the wool Yorkshire who only trusts people North of the Wash. However, she does know it's an illogical prejudice she can do something about, and she is trying," I said.

"Well, I'm relieved to hear that it's not personal at least, but I can tell you I am not posh. I might sound it but that's just because we did elocution at the convent I was sent to. I hear the three of you talking about your families and because I can't join in, I tend to keep quiet, I know it looks as if I'm being stand offish, but I'm not really."

"But why can't you join in with us?" I asked.

Lizzy took a while to answer.

"To be honest my parents don't have much time for me. They dote on my soldier brother and think I should be making 'a good marriage'. I can tell you there is no chance of that in the near future."

"Delia told us you really wanted to go to Art school" I said.

"That's true, but they wouldn't hear of it, 'God knows what kind of people you would meet there, unsuitable types for sure' was what my mother said, so I gave in and agreed to teacher training just so I could get away from home."

"It must have been hard growing up in that sort of atmosphere," I said

"It was but I suppose I knew nothing different, I accepted it. I thought all families were like mine with parents who had to work so hard they had to send me to boarding school to be looked after as well as educated."

"It makes me think of how lucky I am," I said.

We walked on slowly with our own thoughts. As we neared the Smithy, Lizzy went on ahead to check we would be able to get Daisy sorted. I knew she would be able to dazzle anyone into giving her what she wanted.

"He's fine about it but we will have to pay." Said Lizzy

We led Daisy into the yard in front of the Smithy. There was just about enough room for the caravan. We unshackled her.

"She's a bit of a big beast for youse to handle." Said the Smithy

"Yes but she's gentle," I replied, feeling the need to stand up for 'the beast'.

"Well one of youse will have to hold her head collar while I shoe her."

None of us were keen so we ended up drawing straws and I lost.

"Okay I'll do it," I said. I would much rather have watched the operation, knowing that I probably would never have the chance again to see a horse being shod. But actually, I was beginning to feel a bit fond of the old mare so I held the head collar and re-assured Daisy as the smithy started to work.

Half an hour later we were back on the road, having paid him from the kitty purse and getting a receipt.

"Just like on the telly," Kate said about the experience of watching Daisy being shod.

"Well at least I have a souvenir," I said examining the old shoe the Smith had agreed to give me.

Delia offered to walk with Daisy and this time I let her, I felt she might also need a good listener.

"Its three o'clock now and we still have a long way to go, come on Daisy, gee up a bit." I said as I handled the reins for the first time.

I knew the horse would go at her own rate, no matter what I said.

“I think we should call her the Ploddy horse,” I said, feeling suddenly inspired.

“That’s a great idea," said Lizzy

“I like it,” said Kate, “And when we get really mad with her then she is the Bloody Ploddy Horse.” The three of us laughed.

The most annoying result of this slow pace was the number of passers by who made comments. Lizzy and Kate, sitting on the front seats, talking in a variety of accents, thanked them for their concern.

Two more people claimed ownership of Ploddy, her name now Mary and even Snowy. These previous owners were horrified that she was working so hard. I was not so sure that she was.

The most irritating, however, was when someone remarked, “That horse needs a drink!”

To be honest it wasn’t anything we had thought about. I guess we all assumed that she would be accessing a trough when she was free of us, but we couldn’t be sure.

“Delia, do you think Ploddy is thirsty?” I said.

“I’ve absolutely no idea Tess, but we can look out for a stream and see if she wants a drink.”

“Isn’t there a saying, you can take a horse to water but you can’t make it drink?” I said.

After a short while we came to a slow moving stream.

"Let’s find out if it’s true," said Delia, leading the horse to the stream which was just about accessible. Ploddy was not interested.

“Obviously not thirsty," said Delia but I was not so sure.

After three more passers by made comment, I brought the caravan to a halt just before a bridge which crossed a fast running stream.

"Maybe she needs really fresh water," I said. "We can get some here."

I took the bucket stored at the back of the caravan and went down the steep bank to the water below. After struggling back up the slope I offered it to Ploddy who lapped it greedily.

"See, she really is thirsty, I'll get some more."

By the time I had gone up and down to the stream three times I was exhausted.

Delia took over and even after her three journeys up and down Ploddy was still lapping away at each bucketful.

"Who's next?" I asked, looking at Kate and Lizzy.

"I'll do it," said Kate and she jumped down and took the bucket.

She had just started down the slope when Ploddy began to piss... and piss... and piss.

"It's like a bloody torrent," shouted Lizzy, "thirsty my eye! Kate don't bother with any more water, looks like she has had more than enough, she's really taking the piss."

We laughed.

"Delia are you still happy walking with the bloody horse?" I asked.

"Don't you mean Ploddy horse," said Kate.

I filled Delia in on the earlier conversation.

"I like the name," said Delia it certainly suits her, I'd like to carry on walking with Ploddy. Actually I find it really restful, and it gives me time to think." Said Delia

"I know what you mean," I said taking up the reins.

"We really need to get a move on if we are to get to Brennans farm tonight, and as it's the nearest one we have no choice," said Kate.

"Why don't you and Tess go ahead and do the shopping?" suggested Lizzy. "Then we won't have to stop. Wait outside the shop and we will pick you up."

It was a good suggestion so Kate and I set off. We walked in hope as we had no idea how far it was to the next shop, but it did give us a chance to talk.

"Tell me the truth Kate, are you enjoying this holiday?" I said.

"I think we've had a few bad moments and even less good ones. I don't know, maybe I expected too much and I keep thinking it was unfair to expect you to come."

"It was my choice," I said, "I have to admit I have thought I shouldn't have come, but I know it would be even worse at home. There's such a space in the house, and the family don't talk. I think they are afraid of upsetting each other. Dad spends hours just looking out the window and my brothers and sisters seem to be getting on with their own lives. I feel myself on the verge of tears all the time, and if I go out I have to endure people being nice to me. No-one needs to tell me how great my Mam was, I know it."

Kate took my arm. "They're just doing what they can, and they are sorry for your pain. There's nothing they can say that will really make you feel better and they know it. I guess they don't want to ignore you, they do care – just like I do." She squeezed my arm.

"Thanks Kate."

We walked in silence for a while.

"And what are we having for tea tonight?" I asked.

"Let's find a fish and chip shop. I'm sure the other two will be happy with that and we can eat while we are on the move," said Kate. I agreed this was a good idea.

"I've noticed you're trying harder with Lizzy," I said, "I'm sure when you get to know her better, her accent won't get to you as much. You have to admit it was a laugh today with the Americans."

"Yes, it was fun. I guess I can't help being from Yorkshire any more than she can help being from London. Maybe she'll visit Yorkshire one day and then she will understand why it's called God's own country," she said and laughed. "And I have to admit London has a lot going for it too."

The idea of fish and chips went down well, and very fortunately there was a fish and chip shop in the next village. We stopped briefly to make a brew and then resumed the journey to Oughterard. Despite our early start the activities of the day had taken up the time, and dusk was beginning to draw in.

By the time we got to Brennans farm it was getting dark. The farmer was not very welcoming, probably because he had finished for the day but amid much muttering he led Daisy off for the night.

As we seemed to be in the middle of nowhere we settled down with the vodka, orange and playing cards. We only managed an hour.

"It must be all the fresh country air but I am exhausted even though it is only ten o'clock," said Kate and I agreed. Delia was already asleep.

"I don't mind the occasional early night," said Lizzy, "but I hope we are going to have some fun as well."

"Depends what you mean by fun," I said.

"Oh, music, drinking and boys, that sort of fun," said Lizzy, and she laughed.

"You know something Lizzy, I have to agree with you. Let's talk about it tomorrow," said Kate.

"At last they seemed to be agreeing about something," I thought. "Maybe Delia will feel a bit better tomorrow."

I fell asleep, not thinking of myself or my troubles.

Chapter Five -Tuesday

The sun was not out next morning, and it wasn't just drizzling but raining hard. I got up and put the kettle on. None of us had slept well, due mainly to the braying donkey which seemed to be right next to the caravan. All of us had shouted at him at some point during the night.

I thought the farmer had put it there because we had arrived so late. I was debating whether to say something when we heard someone coming down the track. I stuck my head out the door.

"Youse'll want some fresh milk and here are a few eggs for your breakfast. Let me know when you're ready to harness up the horse."

"Thank you very much Mr Brennan and sorry again about arriving so late last night." I said.

"I expect Kathleen kept you awake," was his response.

I looked puzzled.

"The donkey, named after my wife," he explained. I remained puzzled.

"I'll be away now, come and find me at the house if you need me."

Feeling guilty, I thanked him for his kindness and started making breakfast. Delia and Kate got up and dressed.

Lizzy sat up, looked out the window and declared: "I'm not getting up just to get soaked out there."

The atmosphere changed from fed up to something more brittle. Lizzy was only saying how we all probably felt but Kate snapped.

"So what are you going to do? Lie in bed all day? I don't think so. It's about time you pulled your weight here, first you can't cook and you have never once offered to help with the Ploddy horse."

Once she had started at Lizzy, Kate couldn't stop.

"I don't really know why you came on this holiday, you and Delia have been as miserable as sin since we started out. It may not be what any of us expected but we're here now, so why can't you just try and make the most of it?"

"What like you, you mean," said Lizzy. "I've had to listen to you ordering us about, swearing under your breath at me 'the bloody southerner. If you must know I came on this holiday to get away from arguments and being ordered what to do! I have enough of that at home. Now let me get out of here, I need a pee."

Pulling on some clothes, Lizzy flustered her way out of the door.

"Great start to the day Kate," I said. "What's wrong with you this morning? I thought we were just starting to get on yesterday. I don't think you need to be so nasty, besides, you know Lizzy has a point about your attitude towards her, I've tried to tell you about your prejudice."

Kate was close to tears as she sat herself down. "I know, I know, look I am really sorry, both of you. Maybe it's the rain, the donkey, or lack of sleep. I am feeling so bad about this holiday, everything seems to be going wrong and I feel responsible for persuading you to come," said Kate.

"Kate, it's not your fault that things have gone wrong. We are all grownups here, and you are not responsible for our decisions. We have our own reasons to be here, Lizzy too," said Delia.

I agreed with Delia and I believed Kate, she really does feel bad about things, when she can't work out how to make it all better, but I said nothing and got on with my breakfast.

Eventually Lizzy returned and it was obvious she had been crying. I handed her a cup of coffee. Kate went and sat beside her.

"Look, Lizzy I am really sorry for having a go at you, everything just got to me. The donkey, the horse, the weather; but you don't deserve to be the scapegoat for me feeling bad and I promise to try harder to swallow my Yorkshire pride."

Lizzy nodded "And I'll try to pull my weight, as you put it. But I really need to tell you I hate having to go behind bushes to pee. Please can we find somewhere to wash properly, sit down on a toilet and have some fun?"

Kate laughed unexpectedly.

"Didn't know sitting on a toilet could be fun Lizzy, but I know what you mean. That's clearly something we should try and do today," said Kate

"Any ideas what else we can do?" I asked.

Delia, Lizzy and I looked at Kate.

"I haven't a bloody clue," she laughed, still trying to defuse the atmosphere she had created.

"I have an idea," said Delia. She produced the map supplied with the caravan. "Look," she said, "if we go back to Moycullen and take this road towards Galway, we could find somewhere to stay nearer the city. Then we would be able to find a bit of life and hopefully a bit of fun."

"Delia, that's a really great idea," said Kate, "and, before I forget I should apologise to you too for what I said earlier."

"Apology accepted, although I will admit to appearing a bit miserable. If you try to stop being so Yorkshire, I will try to be more cheerful," said Delia

"Agreed," said Kate.

"And now, thanks to your idea Delia, we have something to be cheerful about," I said, looking at the others.

There was an inkling of a smile on their faces. Delia's plan agreed, we prepared to move on.

Kate and I walked up to the farm, it was still raining but not cold. We thanked and paid the farmer's wife, whom, I told Lizzy, was called Kathleen, then collected Ploddy. Before long we were getting the horse ready for another day's work. Mr Brennan arrived to help us.

"Youse can call me Seamus now," he said "where are you off to today? North it'll be raining a bit longer, South the sun will be out soon."

"Good thing we're heading south then," said Kate.

In no time we had Ploddy harnessed up. Delia and Lizzy finished clearing the breakfast things and packing away the bedding.

It was not raining so hard now, but the sky was grey and overcast and there was a heavy drizzle.

"I'll walk with the horse this morning," said Kate, "call it penance, especially if it rains."

"Don't be so miserable Kate, things can only get better," I said, then called to the others, "Ready to roll."

Mr Brennan (call me Seamus) waved us off.

"Say good bye to Kathleen for us," I said. He smiled.

As Kate was feeling conciliatory, I let her walk Daisy even though I would have been happy to. I offered to take the reins.

"No way am I being loo roll monitor," said Lizzy.

"Nor me," I said but pointed out we didn't really need one as the rain was washing away any droppings from the bar at the back of the shafts (the back bar, as we were now calling it).

Delia had disappeared inside with her book.

Lo and behold Daisy quickened her pace, she was almost trotting.

"She probably thinks she's going home," said Lizzy.

"I wish I was," flashed across my brain, I knew it was not a good idea to pursue this line of thought, so changed the subject.

"Great company you two are," I said "since you don't want a conversation, how about a song?"

Lizzy looked at me, then without any pre-amble she started.

"Four wheels on my wagon and I'm just rolling along, the Cherokees are after me but I'm singing a happy song..."

It wasn't exactly difficult to pick up. Kate turned and looked open mouthed at us but soon joined in. Delia left her book and joined us at the front of the van. We spent the next hour putting our own words to the song. I thought the best contribution was from Lizzy, it was so heartfelt!

"One wheel on my wagon and I'm not rolling along,
I found a loo, am sitting here,
Pouring down but I have no fear,
Cos I'm singiiiiing a happy song."

Once started, we carried on singing, mostly songs from the folk club - Liverpool Lou, The summertime is Coming, Kevin Barry and the like. After a good hour of singing I was feeling a lot better and I'm sure the others did too. It had even stopped raining and there was a bit of sunshine.

We reached Moycullen about lunchtime but we had been so busy enjoying ourselves we missed the turn to the Galway road.

From our experience with peat bog man we knew turning round with a horse and caravan isn't easy. We had been advised by Mr McKeown if we needed to do this, then we should unharness the horse, turn the caravan by hand and harness up again. For us to turn round we would have to go right through the town, and find somewhere with enough space to perform the manoeuvre, we decided not to do it. Instead we would drive through the one and only petrol station.

It was going to be tricky, but we reckoned we could just about fit under the canopy, past the pumps and out the other end. None of us were proving to be skilled in driving so we drew straws, Delia won, or perhaps better to say, lost. Kate and I walked Daisy, and Lizzy took up the rear to ensure the wheels were going straight.

"We'll take it slowly," said Kate as we turned Daisy into the forecourt and towards the pumps. At this point the proprietor came flying out.

"What do youse want girls? Want me to fill her up?" He laughed heartily at his own joke.

Delia and Lizzy were distracted just enough for the back end of the caravan to collide with one of the pumps, there was a horrible scraping sound. The owner's sense of humour disappeared rapidly.

"Jesus, look at what you've done. Youse'll have to pay for this, I'll call the Garda."

He didn't have to call loudly as just at that moment the Garda pulled up.

He strolled toward us, taking in the situation and trying not to laugh.

"Hold on now, what's happened here?"

"Look at that, just look at it," the pump was leaning ominously, "a hundred that'll cost me."

Kate and I were speechless, a hundred pounds. Oh my God!

Lizzy was the first to get over the shock, she walked towards the Garda.

"Hello Officer, this is terrible we were just trying to turn the caravan round here. Is it really that bad, the caravan doesn't seem to be much damaged, so surely we couldn't have hit it that hard?" She smiled at him but there was the glint of tears in her eyes.

The Garda melted.

"Look Paddy, isn't this the same pump those Yanks hit a week ago, did you get it fixed right? I believe you got a hundred out of them."

Paddy knew he had been caught out.

"Ach well, it's just the outside is damaged, the pump will be all right, on you go girls you gave us a bit of a laugh, but don't come back."

"Don't worry about that," said Kate as she started to lead Daisy back on to the road. I had noticed that Delia was quite upset and crying real tears so went to help her with the driving.

"Thank you officer, don't know what we would have done without you," said Lizzy with a coy smile.

"That's all right girls but keep out of trouble now."

I could tell he liked being called Officer, especially by Lizzy.

The turn completed, we set off towards the Galway Road.

I had taken over the reins from Delia who was now sobbing inconsolably.

"I'm so sorry, I shouldn't have got so distracted," she wailed.

"But Delia we all were when Paddy came running out, and he was the one in trouble with the Garda, not us. It's not that bad, honestly," I said.

"Oh but it is, it is," and she sobbed even harder.

I called to Lizzy who was walking the horse with Kate.

"Can you come and talk to Delia, she's really upset?"

Lizzy climbed into the caravan.

"It's all right Delia, it wasn't your fault. We'll be laughing about this soon."

Delia cried even more.

"What's wrong Delia, it's not just this, is it?" said Lizzy.

Delia shook her head.

"I think I'm pregnant," she replied.

"Oh my God," said Lizzy and I together.

Both Delia and Lizzy were weeping now!

"Shall we stop," I asked. It was getting close to lunch time anyway.

"Yes," said Lizzy, "I could do with a drink, even if it's only coffee. What about you?" she asked Delia who had now stopped crying.

"Yes please, now I've said it out loud I feel a bit better," said Delia.

I called to Kate to stop at the next convenient place. She clearly knew there was something happening so didn't question the demand.

The next lay-by wasn't that far and Kate was soon leading us off the road. We gathered in the caravan, although I was keeping an eye on Daisy and had hold of her reins, just in case.

Lizzy had put the kettle on.

"What's happened?" asked Kate. "God, Delia but you look awful, have you been crying?"

"I think I might be pregnant Kate," said Delia.

"Oh no!" said Kate, "are you sure?"

"Well I've missed two periods and I am usually very regular," said Delia.

"Was it with John?" asked Lizzy.

I guessed this must be the regular boyfriend she had told us about.

"Do you want to talk about this now Delia?" asked Kate softly.

"It's a relief I've told somebody, but I'd really prefer to talk later. What I would like to do now is just lie down, I've hardly slept the last couple of nights," said Delia.

Lizzy handed out the coffees but Delia declined and went and lay down at the back of the caravan.

"What shall we do now?" I asked.

"Bloody men," muttered Kate.

Although it was lunchtime none of us were hungry.

"Let's just keep heading to the farm we are staying at, and we can decide when we get there," said Lizzy, "I can't think straight right now."

Chapter Six -Tuesday afternoon

I took over from Kate at leading Ploddy. I was glad of the silence and for once I wasn't thinking of myself. What a mess Delia was in. I began to think of girls, including family members who had been through the same. Most of them were supported, however reluctantly, by their families. The majority of those I knew went away to have their baby. Some went to relatives, often in Ireland, but the unlucky ones went to the Diocesan Mothers and Babies home. There were plenty of awful stories about that place. The girls came back after their delivery, on their own, the baby having been sent for adoption or sometimes taken in by another family member. However, the shame and guilt seldom left, both the girl herself and her family. As for the man involved, unless there was hasty wedding I rarely knew who it was. The gossip if there was any was always about the girl. Why did the men always seem to get away scot free? It was definitely worse for a college girl, they were expected to know and behave better. The really sad thing was that love seems to rarely come into it.

"Wake up Tess," Kate shouted, "You're miles away, we are near the junction now, need to turn right don't we?"

Kate was right, I was so lost in thought I hadn't noticed how far we had travelled.

"Yes," I called back, "can someone come and help with Ploddy?"

Lizzy came down and walked on the other side of the horse. After this morning's episode we needed to ensure we were not distracted, especially as we were turning on to a main road. Fortunately it wasn't busy and we could see clearly in both directions, we turned safely. It soon became apparent, however, that we would have to pay a lot more attention to the much faster traffic. For the first time I felt a bit nervous walking Ploddy. Cars were overtaking us, even buses and lorries, and I didn't like it.

I was glad Lizzy had stayed with Ploddy and I.

"How far do we have to go?" I asked Lizzy.

"I was just looking at the map and addresses we have, the nearest place we can stop is Green Farm, about three miles from that last road junction," she said, "not that far out of Galway."

"I think we can manage that," I said.

When we were not holding up traffic it wasn't too bad, most people waved and smiled at us, particularly children and everyone was very patient.

"I feel a bit famous," called Kate, "with everyone gawping at us."

I laughed, and then gasped as we were overtaken by a car with large caravan, it was within inches of our van, and had not slowed down much.

"That was much too close," I said, surprised yet pleased with Ploddy's non reaction.

"Next turning on the right," called Kate.

"I know we normally ask the landowners permission before going on his land but we can't just stop and wait on this road, turn off first and I will go and ask," said Lizzy.

We waited till the road was clear before starting the turn into Green Farm. There was actually a sign with the name of the farm. The entrance was marked by two large wrought iron gates attached to pillars. It was strange that the wall then attached to the pillars on the other side was so low, about three feet high compared to eight feet pillars.

Delia came out to help.

Things were going well, Lizzy guided on one side, I held Ploddy's head collar, Delia guided on the other side and Kate held the reins. All was going according to plan, then calamity struck. A car travelling too fast approached from the left, and Lizzy instinctively stepped into the middle of the road to slow him down. Meanwhile we, as before, were distracted enough for the caravan to go off centre.

The sill above the wheels of the caravan caught the bottom hinge of the open gate, lifting the gate almost off the hinge. As the gate teetered at an angle, one of the spikes along the top caught the canvas cover of the van and ripped it. There was a commotion of noise, tearing, shouting, grating, screeching brakes all in confusion. Ploddy came to an abrupt halt. The four of us stood and swore, cursed and wept. The worst casualty was the gate. It was seriously unstable, and the pillar it was now only half attached to was definitely wobbling. The only good thing was that we were at least off the road.

The car, which had been the cause of our distraction, stopped and the two male occupants, realising the trouble we were in, came to help. There was no apology forthcoming.

"We have to get that gate back on quick before the whole bloody lot falls down," said one of the men.

"Come on, space out along the width of this gate, and on a count of three, everybody lift."

We, still in shock, did as we were bid.

"One, two, three, lift," we called in unison, managing to lift the gate back onto its hinge. The pillar seemed a bit more stable.

With the immediate danger being dealt with, we turned to the caravan. There seemed to be no real damage to the sill, but the canvas now flapping in the breeze exposed the flimsy hardboard which formed the curved roof of the van.

"Dieter won't be too happy about the gate," said one of our helpers.

"Who's Dieter?" asked Kate.

"The farmer, he's German and a good man, lots of German landowners round here," said the other helper.

"Don't worry about the rip, a bit of tape will fix it for youse. Come on Joe, we need to be going. Bye girls and if you feel like drowning your sorrows meet you in Paddy's Place tonight!" They drove off.

"Thanks very much, you pair of clowns." Kate shouted as they sped away, "first they nearly run into us then offer not a word of apology, and drive off."

"They did help us with the gate," I said, but she was not in a forgiving mood and I didn't blame her, if they hadn't been driving so fast this wouldn't have happened.

"Let's move away from the gate and we can look at the damage to the caravan," said Lizzy.

We were at the end of a wide, long drive which curved uphill a few hundred yards ahead of us. We couldn't see any buildings and assumed they were up the hill. On each side of the drive was grass, recently cut. I led Ploddy onto the verge on our left, there was plenty of space for the caravan beside a well maintained stone wall.

We all examined the damage more closely. If we could pull the ripped edges together we could affect a temporary repair with some large safety pins, I suggested.

"Well at least we are near the city so should be able to buy something we can use to repair it." said Kate, "It's not raining or too windy, hopefully it won't get any worse."

"What are we going to tell the farmer?" I asked. "He's on his way down." They turned and we watched as he came down the drive towards us.

"We can't tell him the truth, we just can't afford to pay for the damage to the gate pillar," said Kate.

"We'll have to act normal, as if we know nothing," said Lizzy," whatever that means," she added.

"Right," said Delia, "smile and lie, I'm good at that." She didn't look very happy and then she pasted on a smile. "Come on the rest of you, we can do this."

"Hello, hello," he waved as he came towards us, he seemed friendly.

"Welcome girls, to my farm, please call me Dieter."

"Thank you," replied Kate, "we've only just arrived, how did you know we were here?"

"I didn't, just on my way across the top there, when I saw you." He waved towards the top of the hill. I think we were all wondering exactly how much he had seen, I know I was. Lizzy was on the ball.

"We were just deciding who was going to come and find you, and who was going to see to the horse. I'm sorry we couldn't ask you before coming onto your land but the road was so busy we couldn't stop."

Surely if he had seen anything this was the moment to mention it, but he didn't.

"Ach girls it is fine, I know the road. If you go up to the farm my wife will sell you some milk and eggs. I will take the mare into the next field, the gates are open here and we don't want her running away."

"Chance would be a fine thing," I thought.

"Yes, we noticed the gates," said Kate brazenly.

He hadn't seen anything, I thought, but I couldn't look at the others.

He offered to unharness Ploddy, but Kate and I insisted we could do it.

"What happened here?" he said, pointing at the ripped canvas.

"Oh that," said Lizzy, "we had a very near miss with a caravan, it was overtaking us too fast and too close, something sticking out caught our canvas."

"Did he stop?" asked Dieter.

"No, I don't even know if he knew what had happened, and we were not quick enough to get his number. Is it far to Galway from here? We were thinking of going to get some stuff to make a repair."

"God," I thought, "she is such a cool liar!"

"Only a few miles, there's a bus every hour and the bus stop just out of the gates on the left" said Dieter.

We fed Ploddy her oats then he took her off.

"I will put her in the paddock just next to you," he said.

"Is there water for her?" I asked.

"Of course," he said.

Delia and Kate went to get the milk and eggs. Lizzy and I made the sandwiches and tea for our delayed lunch. I turned to Lizzy.

"I thought your story about the overtaking caravan was brilliant, it sounded so plausible."

"I'm not so sure," she said, "how could someone do that damage and not know about it, and we still have the gate pillar to worry about."

"I know, right now I feel like running away from all this..." Lizzy cut me short.

"That's a great idea, why don't we have our lunch and then go into Galway, we can have our tea there later, and then go to Paddy's Place, the Bar those lads told us about"

"I'm not so sure I want to see those two again," I said, "but I think going to Galway for our tea is a great idea and I'm sure there are plenty of bars we could visit. I'm certain Kate will be up for it, what do you think about Delia?"

"We'll ask," said Lizzy.

It wasn't long before Delia and Kate arrived back from the farmhouse, they told us how they had been welcomed warmly, which made them both feel worse.

"What a day," said Kate, "it's just been one thing after another."

We sat at the table with tea and sandwiches. It was about 4.30pm

"Actually," said Delia, "I was just thinking it's been a good day for me, at least this afternoon has, being able to share things with you all may have been hard because I can't pretend any more. But it's been such a relief at the same time."

"What happened, Delia?" asked Lizzy. "I thought you and John finished a few months ago?"

"We did, John finished with me and I didn't see it coming so I was pretty upset, then I met Rob. It was a rebound thing, nice enough guy but I knew it wasn't real for me, if you know what I mean." We nodded. "We were both reckless, I guess. I stopped seeing him after it happened."

"After what happened?" said Lizzy.

"Neither of us were experienced, the condom split, I got pregnant, ruined my life... How am I going to tell my Mum and Dad, not just that I'm pregnant but that I will be thrown out of college?"

She started weeping again.

"How many periods have you missed?" asked Kate.

"Two," said Delia, "and the chemist confirmed it just before I came on holiday."

Lizzy held her friends hand.

I didn't know what to say, we all knew Delia was right, she would be thrown out of college, it had happened to other students and there was no forgiveness from the nuns or the church.

"We know what this means for you Delia," said Kate, "I just wish there was something I could do or say to make you feel better but the truth is I can't."

"Thanks Kate, thanks all of you. I know you understand, and in my heart I know my parents will support me whatever happens, it's just that the future I had planned has changed to one I haven't. I don't even know if I want to keep the baby, it wasn't conceived in love after all," said Delia.

"Delia, I know you." said Lizzy, "you are strong and will cope with whatever happens. Your family are loving and supportive and I am here to help you in any way I can. Right now none of us can do anything to change things, but we are on holiday, in a beautiful part of the world. What about going into Galway for the evening? It would do you and us all good to see a bit more than the back of the Ploddy horse."

Delia smiled: "I don't know if I am up to it but you three go, I know you want to see a bit more of Ireland."

"Don't be ridiculous Delia, we're not leaving you here," said Kate and I almost together.

"Kate, you and Tess go, I'll stay with Delia," said Lizzy. "Let's go outside Delia and give these two space to get ready."

I reluctantly changed my shirt, Kate and I decided to wear the Fishermans tops she had brought for each of us. Unusually we spoke very little, and the silence was broken when Lizzy re-appeared.

"Delia has changed her mind, she's coming with us," she said.

I don't know what she had said to make Delia change her mind but I felt so pleased that she had. This was a time for us to band together. When we were ready Kate and I waited outside and soon Delia and Lizzy appeared, wearing the Fishermans tops, 'solidarity' I thought feeling happy.

"Don't forget your wash things," said Kate. "We'll find a sink with hot water somewhere."

We were soon heading for the bus stop. As we passed through the gates we looked guiltily at the unstable pillar, the gate itself was undamaged.

"Forget it for now, there's nothing we can do. Can you see the bus stop?" I said.

We soon found it and while we waited Delia looked at the timetable.

"Last bus back is 10 o'clock," she said.

"Come on Delia, we're forgetting our troubles, remember. We'll worry about getting home when the time comes," said Lizzy squeezing her friend's hand.

Delia smiled and said no more. The bus arrived soon after, and we enjoyed the short journey into Galway. The one thing of note was the new Cathedral which had been recently consecrated with much pomp and ceremony. Within half an hour we were in the city.

We split into our pairs and walked round the busy streets. I found it exhilarating to be back among lots of people. I thought we might find a shop that sold pins and tape for the canvas repair but all the practical type shops were closed.

We found a tearoom which had a toilet with sink where we could get a wash. As we were not customers only Kate and I washed there. Lizzy and Delia used the toilet in the pub next door. Feeling cleaner and fresher we window shopped for a while then went to find somewhere to eat. Although we were not that hungry after a late lunch.

"Look," said Kate, "there's one of those new Pizza places, let's give it a try."

It felt very sophisticated to me, I loved it. We just had one between the four of us and agreed to get some chips later.

Over our pizza Delia put forward an idea.

"At home when I go out with friends we like to make up a story about ourselves, just for a laugh. Sometimes I tell lads I'm a writer or training to be a doctor. If I really want to get rid of them I tell them I'm training to be a missionary."

We nodded, we had all played that game until we got caught out. But we had a good laugh about it later.

Kate had an inspired thought.

"Why don't we pretend to be novice nuns enjoying our last bit of freedom before we enter the convent?"

"That's a great idea," said Lizzy.

"Yes," I said, "we're wearing a sort of habit, and we certainly know about nuns."

Our story agreed, we applied a bit of make-up and set out to find somewhere to have a drink, there were plenty of bars.

"Look" said Kate 'Paddy's Place' "Isn't that where those two idiots who caused our accident said they would be? Definitely not going there."

We strolled on and came to 'Ryans Bar', it seemed popular so we joined the crowd going in. Once inside we could feel the atmosphere almost straight away, excitement was in the air, it was fantastic. It was an enormous space with a long bar down one side of the room, live music from somewhere at the other end. Laughter, and calls to the bar staff, filled the air. The place was packed, but we managed to stick together till we reached the bar. Wearing the smock tops was a good idea, it marked us out as something different. The men at the bar stood aside for us. Kate took out the kitty purse, she and I had a pint of Guinness, and I was surprised when Delia asked for a half, while Lizzy stuck to her usual vodka and lime. Then the craic started...

"Well what have we here? Haven't seen you around, on holiday are youse?"

"What's that you're wearing? It looks like a uniform."

"Where are you from girls? You look English."

Kate answered.

"Yes we are, just here on holiday before we enter the convent."

There was a roar of laughter.

"Oh my God, nuns and Guinness, and what order would that be?"

"Oh it's an English order, Sisters of St Susan," said Delia.

"St Susan, doesn't sound saint like to me," said one of the lads.

"Shame on you," said Delia, "have you never heard of St. Susannah?"

"No, but they let you out to party, very generous of them..."

And so it went on, the wisecracks getting funnier with every drink.

A new guy joined us.

"Well hello girls, and how's the horse? Still alive I hope. Unless of course you've poked its eyes out by now."

It was Dermott, our saviour from the first day. He winked at Kate. The joke was up.

"Ok we aren't really nuns, we're just four students on holiday with a horse drawn caravan," admitted Delia.

"And the horse is outside is it ?Getting his oats?"

More laughter.

Dermott squeezed himself in next to Kate and stayed there most of the evening. We had to endure him telling of our embarrassing episode and again there was much laughter, this time at our expense, but it didn't matter we were having some fun and it felt great after the trials of the day.

The evening passed quickly then Delia remarked we had missed the last bus, we had missed it by at least an hour in fact.

Although the five or six likely lads who had spent the evening with us had introduced themselves we had trouble remembering their names, all except Dermott.

"Don't worry," he said, "I'll get you back to your caravan as long as you don't mind a squash. I've got Seamus and Connor to take too."

It wasn't too hard to work out who Seamus and Connor were, the ones with the widest smiles at the prospect of being squashed up with us in the back.

Leaving before we got too drunk, we piled into Dermott's Hillman. He insisted Kate sit next to him, and as it was a bench seat Kate insisted I sit with her too. Seamus and Connor sat themselves in the back and made it clear Lizzy and Delia should sit on their laps.

"Sorry boys," said Lizzy, "don't know you well enough for that. Shove up and let us in." Lizzy sparkled when she was being intimidating, and these two stood no chance. They moved over and let Lizzy and Delia into the back seat

"And no groping," added Lizzy. As if they dared.

Lizzy's message had been heard by Dermott, and he kept his eyes on the road and his hands on the wheel.

It took us a little while to find the caravan as of course, it was dark but after a few false stops we arrived at the gates to the farm.

None of us had mentioned the events of the day, it still felt too raw, and seeing the gate again was a reminder.

"Can we come in for a drink," chanced Connor.

"No not tonight," said Kate, "we've had a busy day haven't we?"

She made sure of eye contact with each of us, none of us wanted a late night.

The boys drove off but not before telling us about the Show band appearing tomorrow night.

"The best in the West," said Dermott, "it'll be a grand night."

"We'll see how we feel," replied Kate, but I saw her smile as she turned and got out of the car.

The boys drove off, and we linked arms as we walked the short distance to the van.

No need for a nightcap tonight, we were exhausted physically and emotionally and were into our beds as quickly as possible. Despite the hardness and the lack of width, I felt sure I would sleep better tonight.

As we settled down in the dark Delia called softly: "Thanks girls, I'm glad I've told you about the baby. I feel so much better not having to hold on to that secret."

"That's all right Delia," Lizzy answered, "we all know about secrets. Sleep well."

Chapter Seven -Wednesday Morning

We slept late the next day knowing we weren't going anywhere. The sun was out and it was warm, if it hadn't been for the gate disaster at least three of us would be feeling good. We enjoyed a tasty breakfast courtesy of Mrs Dieter who had provided us with eggs, bread, milk and a little pot of marmalade at a very reasonable price. As we sat at the table with the door open we saw Dieter approaching on the path from the farmhouse.

"Do you think he is coming to see us," asked Delia.

"Remember if he asks, we were hit by a caravan and for God's sake don't mention the gate," said Lizzy. "In fact let me do the talking."

I could see that Kate was not too pleased with this but we had no time to argue.

"Good morning girls, lovely day for you," Dieter said as he approached the caravan.

"Thank you," we replied trying to smile innocently. As he drew level we expected him to stop but he didn't, he carried on walking down the path towards the gate. Kate quietly leaned out and watched him while reporting back to us.

"He's walking down the path, there's a car, someone is handing him something, the car is driving off. He is looking at the pillar, now at the gate and again at the pillar. Oh God now he is pushing it, he's looking this way, he's coming back."

Kate ducked back inside, she was pale. "What are we going to say? We can't afford..."

Lizzy interrupted, "Say nothing," she hissed. "Act nonchalant, now who wants another coffee?"

I got a fit of nervous giggles at thinking of ways we could act nonchalantly, draped over our beds perhaps?

Kate glared at me and I soon shut up.

Minutes later Dieter appeared at the door.

"Girls what do you know about the gate post?"

As she had instructed we left it to Lizzy.

"The gate post? Is there something wrong?"

"It looks as if something has hit it, was it you?"

"Us! I think we would have known if we had, it's a pretty substantial gate."

Dieter gave Lizzy a long look and then walked round the caravan examining the wheels.

"What's this?" he said pointing at a very clear scratch on the back wheel arch.

"Oh that's from something that happened in Moycullen the other day."

Delia joined in: "Yes we had to turn round, and unfortunately hit the pump at the petrol station where we were manoeuvring.

It was very embarrassing because there was a Garda parked nearby who saw it happen."

Another long look from Dieter.

"We did hear a crunching sound when we were having our tea last night, before we went out. Didn't we?" This came from Kate, looking round at us.

I felt as if I was being directed in some sort of play, an improvisation in which we all had to take a part, so I added my piece.

"Yes, and when we looked out we saw a lorry driving away from the gate but we didn't actually see it hit it." Now it was my turn for the long look.

"Hmph," muttered Dieter as he walked back up towards the farm house. We remained silent until we were sure he was out of earshot.

"Do you think he believed us?" asked Delia.

"I doubt it very much but without a witness he can't prove it was us," replied Lizzy.

"I feel bad about it, he and his wife have been so nice to us," I added.

"I know," said Kate. "Don't let us dwell on it, we should get the canvas fixed as well as we can and then get ready for a night out."

"Ok I'll leave you to it. I'm going to see how the horse is," said Lizzy. Collecting her sketch pad she set off up the path towards the field where Ploddy was.

"Honestly," said Kate, "who does she think she is, 'leaving us to it'. When does she not leave us to it?"

I couldn't believe it, last night we were getting on so well and I really felt we had pulled together to support Delia, who was, at this moment, obviously on my wave length.

"Oh for God's sake Kate, shut up," said Delia, "I'm fed up with your snide comments about Lizzy. You hardly know her and clearly don't even want to try and be friends. You may feel at home with your narrow-minded judgements but there are bigger things to worry about than the sound of someone's accent. I'm off for a walk."

Without waiting for a response Delia stalked off after Lizzy.

Kate stood and watched Delia until she was out of sight.

"Let's wash up then see if we have anything we can use to fix this canvas," she said, not looking at me.

The best we could find were a couple of large safety pins. It was better than nothing, I thought, as we pulled the canvas together, at least it's not raining. The hardboard used to form the barrel roof would not be waterproof and the canvas needed to be mended soon before it shrank back away from the tear too much.

"We'll have to find someone to make a better job or get some stuff ourselves, we should go to Galway before the shops close," I said to Kate, who now also seemed to be setting off for a walk.

"Won't be long Tess," she called back to me.

"Well, just great," I thought.

Last night we had all seemed to be moving towards being friends, we'd had quite a laugh. What's happened to us? Once again I wondered why on earth I had come on this holiday, every day brought more trouble. It was turning into a disaster. Just like my life. My dream to work in Canada when I qualified was just a dream after all. How can I leave Dad, he won't be able to manage without Mum, I would just be a poor second.

I tried to distract myself with a book but the tears started again. This time, as there was no-one around, I didn't hold back. Soon I was sobbing hard then I must have slept, for the next thing I remember was Delia gently shaking me awake.

"Wake up Tess," said Delia, "where's Kate?"

I sat up slowly.

"She said she was going for a walk, didn't you see her?"

"No, would probably have gone the other way if I had." She paused and then said: "Do you think I was a bit harsh on her?"

I didn't really know what to say, truthfully I was fed up standing up for my friend when I knew Kate didn't mean half of what she said.

"Look Delia, I know that Kate is coming across as a snob, she has been brought up to think Yorkshire is God's own country and she just hasn't travelled or met enough people from other places to widen her view. You were right in what you said but I know for sure that Kate didn't mean to hurt Lizzy."

"Maybe you are right. Lizzy has been a really good friend to me just as Kate has been for you. It's a shame they are both so pig headed."

"Well, I guess they will put in an appearance soon enough, let's get on with the sandwiches."

Lizzy was the next to return.

"You look happy," said Delia.

"I am, I managed to get some pretty good sketches done. What a difference the sunshine makes."

"Let's have a look then," I asked.

Lizzy handed over her sketch pad.

I leafed through the pad. As well as the new sketches of the horse, there were drawings of the caravan and of Delia, Kate and me. There were even small landscape details and sketches of what I can only call Irish faces.

"I really like this one of Ploddy, you've managed to catch that superior look she has, but they are all really great Lizzy. Didn't you want to go to art school? You obviously enjoy drawing and you have a real talent, you must know that,". I said.

I caught sight of Delia standing behind Lizzy and shaking her head.

"Not everyone thinks like that, but one day maybe I will," said Lizzy, then added quickly: "Is that kettle boiling yet? I'm ready for a cup of tea."

As we stood chatting, Kate approached. Lizzy got in first.

"Good attempt at a repair," she said looking at our effort, the pins were really straining to hold the canvas together.

"It'll do for now but we have to get something stronger than two safety pins. We should get a move on, we need supplies," Kate replied and walked past us into the caravan.

The atmosphere was strained as we ate our sandwich lunch. Delia and I tried to keep things light.

"Should we have our tea in Galway? Then we won't need to come back here to get ready for tonight," I suggested.

"Yes, good idea, we can take our wash things too, but let's find somewhere better than a pub toilet," Delia added.

Kate and Lizzy nodded.

"There's a bus in twenty minutes," said Kate looking at the bus timetable Dieter had given us, "they seem to run every hour."

"Well there's not much to keep us here, let's try and get the next bus," said Lizzy.

We left our mugs and plates in the sink as per usual. There wasn't time for more chat as we each collected what we needed for the evening. Clean top, make up and wash bag, then we hurried to catch the bus. We just made it, arriving at the Stop just as the bus pulled in. It was busy on board and we split up into our pairs.

Kate had been much quieter than usual after her walk and she still seemed preoccupied with her thoughts.

"What's up Kate?" I asked.

"I've been thinking about something Delia said the other day."

"What was that?"

"She said we all had our reasons for being here and she was right as far as I'm concerned and now, because of my selfishness we are having the holiday from hell."

"What are you talking about?"

"You know Tess, I am having second thoughts about Pete. I thought this holiday would give me a chance to think about him, to see if I miss him, and to make a decision about finishing with him."

"And what's the problem with that?"

"I so desperately wanted to have a break from him, and all I seem to have done is make three other people as miserable as I am."

"Stop Kate, we have already discussed this and no-one is blaming you or holding you responsible for what's happened, and anyway it's not all bad. Last night was a laugh wasn't it?"

"I guess so."

"Well tonight is going to be even better. I can feel it in my bones."

Kate smiled.

"By the way," I went on, "are you missing Pete?"

"No, not really, but I still have to decide what I'm going to do about him. He's not a bad man but I am beginning to think he is not the one for me."

"Well, still a couple of days to go, you never know what will happen."

"Is that meant to console me?" she smiled.

"How many more times do I have to tell you, it's not your fault. We all had the information telling us what it would be like." I was getting fed up telling Kate this.

"If I remember rightly it said something about ambling along the tranquil roads of Galway. Stopping at your leisure to enjoy the delicious foods of the area, the wonderful views and friendly people. It didn't mention you had to find your own toilets in bushes and worse, wash in streams or just stand in the rain, not to mention an ancient horse too stubborn to walk more than two miles an hour."

"And what about unsafe walls and other obstacles," I laughed.

"Yes like petrol pumps and gates that just jumped at us. That's what we will tell the owners when we get back to Barna."

"I think we may feel a bit miserable now but in the future we will laugh about it all."

"Yes, you are probably right Tess, thanks for cheering me up a bit. Now I just have to be nice to Lizzy."

The bus dropped us in the centre of Galway and we split up to have a look round.

"Let's decide where we are going to have tea and then we can arrange to meet there," said Lizzy.

"That pizza place we went to last night is somewhere we all know," said Kate.

We agreed to meet there at six, reporting possible places where we could wash and change.

We set off, Kate and I to look for materials to repair the caravan, Lizzy and Delia to have a good look round.

Chapter Eight -Wednesday evening

We met at six as agreed outside the Pizza Palace. Lizzy and Delia had found a hotel with a spacious ladies room where we could wash and change. 'The Paramount' was just round the corner and was, as Delia had described, old fashioned, not crowded, and with hot water in the ladies. The plan was that two of us would sit with a drink, while the other two went to the bathroom for a wash and change of clothes. There were no other women in the bar so we wouldn't be getting strange looks from other customers using the Ladies. Lizzy and Delia went first and came back sweetly smelling and well scrubbed up. Katie and I drained our drinks and went to get ready. Half an hour later we were all heading towards 'Galway's best Fish Restaurant' which Kate and I had spotted earlier.

Once seated we relaxed and talked about our day.

"Did you get the repair stuff?" asked Lizzy.

Kate took out our purchases. Some kind of waterproof adhesive tape and more safety pins, nappy pins actually.

"They didn't really have a section for tarpaulin repairs but the man said this should be okay. The tape is the widest they had, it will look like a grey stripe across the green, could look artistic."

We laughed.

"Should we put one on the other side?" said Lizzy.

"Maybe," smiled Kate. After enjoying and paying for the delicious Fish Tea we counted our kitty money and agreed that, as last night, we would pay for the majority of our own drinks. It was a bit early to go to "Ryan's Bar" so we went for a stroll down to Salthill and the sea. We found a bench and sat for a while enjoying the view and character of the place. People were not in a rush here, they strolled along enjoying the evening sun. There were lots of dog walkers and groups of children playing on the beach. The soothing sound of the waves seemed to have a calming effect on all of us. I couldn't speak for the others but for me this evening was the first time in months I felt really alive and looking forward to whatever came my way.

"I am really looking forward to tonight," I said.

"Me too," said Delia, "this may be my last fling so I am going to make the most of it."

She smiled but there were tears in her eyes.

"Well let's make it a good memory," said Kate.

A sentiment we all agreed with.

We made our way to the venue, 'Ryans Bar'. There were posters everywhere about the Show Band, it looked as if it would be a good night. Before we reached Ryans we stopped at smaller bar for a drink and to make a plan. As we were no longer complete strangers we thought we knew what to expect. The boys will have picked us off, who was going with whom. A reasonable amount of drink would be headed our way, then the craic, innuendos, stories, and blarney leading to relaxation and the real business of the night, physical contact with the opposite sex. As far as I was concerned I would prefer to make the craic last as long as possible with whoever had drawn my straw. I wanted to put off the groping for as long as possible.

"Well they know now we are no nuns," said Lizzy.

"Wish I was," said Delia under her breath.

"I am not expecting to meet Mr. Right here, but we can have some fun. It looks as if the music will be good and there will be a chance to dance. Let's look out for each other and see if we can find someone to give us all a lift home," said Kate and no-one disagreed. Not really much of a plan but we were happy with it.

Dermott was hanging around near the door of Ryans.

"Waiting for anyone?" asked Kate.

"Maybe," he said, "but I'll take youse all in anyway."

Kate looked a bit disappointed, but soon forgot about it, when he produced tickets for the four of us. The place was heaving even though it was only eight o'clock.

"Follow me," said Dermott and we followed his weaving path to the bar. When we arrived there two of the likely lads from last night were getting in the drinks. I was impressed, not only did they remember our names but our preferred drinks too.

Seamus handed me a drink. "Not like last night is it?" he said.

"Is this because of the Band?"

"Yes, wait till you hear them."

"Do you think we'll get a table?" I didn't want to get separated off so early in the evening.

"Connor is sorting it out, we'll have one soon enough," said Seamus.

The other three were nearby being chatted up, obviously the boys had a plan too.

Connor arrived and we followed him to a table squashed at the back of the hall.

Once we were seated and drinking, the craic started and it was great fun. We added our own bit with descriptions of our disastrous holiday. Dermott put his arm round Kate at every chance, he was clearly smitten by her. Connor had latched on to Delia, and was enjoying her company. Seamus was easy to talk to and not bad looking with dark hair and twinkly blue eyes, I had drawn a good straw. However Lizzy and her deemed partner Donal did not seem to be hitting it off so well. Donal was very quiet and clearly intimidated by Lizzy's appearance. We were used to her good looks and I had forgotten that she could actually strike a man dumb, Donal had not been here last night so meeting her for the first time tonight had obviously overwhelmed him. Lizzy joined in with the general chat for a while then left the table. I was enjoying all the wit and banter too much to worry about Lizzy, and then on came the band.

The music was loud and glorious and it was impossible to stay still. We danced and danced, sometimes singing, joining in with the songs we knew. We were loosely dancing with the boys, more as a group than in pairs but inevitably came the slow numbers when we were scooped up and held close.

Seamus and I meandered around the dance floor, I was happy being held and didn't really want to talk, but I could see Kate and Dermott in close discussion. Delia was a bit giggly but eventually calmed down.

The music finished for the interval and the lads joined the surge to the bar while we sat catching up at the table.

"You and Dermott seemed very close," I said to Kate.

She smiled. "Oh, he's full of blarney."

"Ah but good blarney I hope," I said and she blushed.

"Well you and Seamus seem to be getting on well, and you and Connor," she said, drawing Delia in.

"Yes, he's very nice for someone I'll probably never see again, but I'm really enjoying myself, so don't worry about me."

I hadn't seen Lizzy for a while so when the interval came and we rejoined at the table I had expected her to be there.

"What's happened to Lizzy?" I asked Delia but she said she had hardly seen her once the dancing started.

"Kate, what about you, have you seen her?" I said.

"No, but she is not with Donal because he is over there with someone else."

She nodded across to the bar. True enough he was there with his arm around another girl and chatting to his friends.

When they came back to the table I asked Seamus if Donal had said anything about Lizzy.

"He said she was way out of his league and that both of them felt uncomfortable, so they agreed to go their own way."

Just then I saw Lizzy making her way to the table, holding the hand of a very good looking young man.

"This is James," said Lizzy, "he is on holiday too."

"Hello," said James as he glanced around the table.

"Are you enjoying the band?" asked Dermott.

"Great," answered James and before Lizzy could say anything, Kate had linked arms with her, pulling her towards myself and Delia.

"Remember what we discussed earlier about buying our own drinks, it's just not happening and I don't like being bought drinks all night, you know that brings expectations."

"So what are you saying Kate, that we should buy our own? Don't think that will go down well here," said Lizzy.

"Let me finish," said Kate. "I suggest we put our kitty money in with the lads, keeping enough back for a taxi in case we can't get a lift. What do you all think?"

Delia and I agreed.

"You don't need to worry about me," said Lizzy, "James has a car and he has already offered me a lift. It's a sports car so we won't all be able to fit in it. But I'm happy for you to use the kitty for whatever you want. I'll see you later."

She walked over to James and taking his hand led him towards the bar.

"Well that's one less to worry about, "I heard Kate mumble under her breath to no-one in particular . She produced the kitty purse and gave most of the money to Dermott, even after knowing him such a short time, it was clear he was the leader of this group of lads. After a bit of insistence on Kate's part he accepted the money. We had all quite a bit to drink but Delia was living up to her plan, she must have had at least four glasses of cider so far. As soon as the music started up again we were back on the dance floor.

In what seemed no time at all, the band were playing its last Jim Reeves slow number. Kate, Delia and I smooched around the floor with our new friends. There was no sign of Lizzy. There were cheers as the band took their leave and the horrible moment when the lights came on showed the three of us to be slightly the worse for wear.

"Keep together," slurred Kate as we went to retrieve our things.

"Yes Mum," responded Delia, and the remark set me off weeping.

"Oh God Tess I am sorry – I didn't mean to upset you," Delia said.

I couldn't say anything, just shook my head.

"Dermott is sorting out a lift for us," said Kate.

She put an arm around my shoulder and led us towards the door. Delia was stumbling behind us, still apologizing.

Of the six of us, Dermot was the least drunk, and within ten minutes he appeared at the kerb and beckoned to us to get in. Kate got in the front. Unlike last night we were much friendlier with the lads and Delia and I were happy to squeeze up close. The alcohol probably had something to do with it. Taking Lizzy at her word, that she would make her own way back, we set off. Kate gave directions, although Dermott had remembered pretty well where we were camped. We all took for granted that the boys would be staying on for a bit for a nightcap or two. The three lads were curious to see inside the caravan but even more, unbelievably to me, they wanted to see the horse. We, of course, had made her out to be some sort of devil horse, huge, lazy and mean. We waved in the direction of the field next door and were surprised when about fifteen minutes later Connor appeared leading Ploddy.

"Well I wouldn't call her big, and she's certainly not mean, what she needs is a ride."

And without more ado he somehow got on her back, and rode over to us.

"Come on Delia, have you ever ridden bare back before?"

I was shocked as I watched him lean down and pull Delia up to ride behind him.

I guessed it was the drink that made her fearless because even though she had to hang onto Connor she was laughing and whooping just like him.

"God, Kate is she all right?" I said.

"She's fine Tess, and look at Ploddy, have you ever seen her move so fast?"

"You don't need to worry about Delia," said Dermott, "Connor is one of the best horsemen in Galway, and he knows all there is to know about horses."

Connor trotted over and Delia dismounted ungracefully, she was complaining of feeling sick, not that surprising.

Dermott and Seamus each had a ride on Ploddy but it was soon clear she was tired out and they took her back to the field.

"Well that woke me up," said Dermott, "what we all of us need now is a drink." He and Seamus collected a box of beer from the car, while Delia got out our vodka and orange.

Kate and I showed the lads the damage to the tarpaulin.

"I'll try and find some time when I can maybe fix that for youse." said Dermott.

"Really, Dermott? That would be great," replied Kate.

"And when I've done it maybe we could go for a drive?" he said fixing his eye on Kate.

"That would be fab Dermott, we've been here nearly a week but we haven't seen that much of the area. What do you think Tess?" said Kate

"I think it's a great idea Dermott" I said .

"And I am sure the other two would love it." said Kate

I knew perfectly well Dermott's invitation was to Kate alone, but he hadn't known her long enough to be aware of her deviousness. I did.

"Let's have a drink," she said before Dermott could say anything else.

Delia and the lads had started drinking and it wasn't long before the canoodling began.

"I hope Lizzy is okay," I said.

"I thought James seemed to be a gentleman," said Delia, "she'll be fine."

"What about her regular boyfriend back home?" I said.

"And who would that be?" said Delia.

"Never mind about Lizzy, she'll be back soon," muttered Connor, as he wrapped his arms round Delia.

Now paired up we lay down on our single bunks and the serious business began.

I was not in the mood for struggling with wandering hands so told Seamus straight I was okay with kissing and cuddling but that's all.

"Fine with me," he replied. Within minutes he was snoring and I fell asleep to the sound of slurping kisses, low moanings and some rustling of clothes.

Chapter Nine -Thursday Morning

"Tess, Tess, wake up," it was Kate whispering in my ear and gently shaking me.

"What's wrong?"

"It's Delia, get up."

I managed to extricate myself from Seamus' arms.

The sun was just rising but it was still very early.

"She's outside, being sick and in pain."

I clambered out and saw Delia over near the hedge, she was kneeling and clutching her tummy. We rushed over to her.

"What are the pains like Delia? Is it like period cramps," I asked.

"Yes but ten times worse, and I've been sick again."

"That could be the drink," I said, not very helpfully.

"Tess, can you go and get some pads and stuff," instructed Kate.

I returned to the caravan to find the lads just about to leave.

Dermott called to me from the car "See you all tomorrow."

Truthfully I was glad to see them go. I knew what was happening and certainly didn't feel like explaining to them.

When I returned to Delia and Kate, Delia was in tears.

"She's bleeding," said Kate.

We helped Delia back to the caravan.

"How painful are your periods normally, Delia?" asked Kate.

"I usually have bad cramps the first day then I am okay," Delia said.

"It will probably be the same now, although the cramps may be a bit more intense. You know what's happened?" said Kate.

Delia nodded.

"Christ I feel so bad, this is all my own fault, all that booze and then riding the bloody horse. I made it happen didn't I? God it's so sordid." She started weeping again.

I went to put the kettle on for a cup of tea.

"Don't be so hard on yourself Delia, not every pregnancy ends in a birth," said Kate, "it happens to lots of women, it happened to me."

Delia and I looked at Kate who was gazing into the distance.

"When was that?" I asked. Even though I was a close friend I had never heard Kate speak of it.

"It was just before my eighteenth birthday. When I realised I'd missed two periods I went into a panic. I can't tell you how relieved I was when I started bleeding," said Kate.

"That must've been hard for you, but you didn't make it happen. I did."

"Did you really Delia?" I asked. "Did you drink loads because you thought it might bring on a miscarriage? And did you ride the horse for the same reason?"

"No, of course not, I told you I wanted to have a last fling. The consequences of drinking loads didn't occur to me. In fact I had accepted that I would have the baby, and it would probably be adopted. Just yesterday I was planning how I would tell my Mum and Dad."

"There you go then. It was a natural miscarriage and even if you had brought it on you will never know, there's no point worrying about it," said Kate.

I served up three mugs of tea.

"That doesn't make me feel any better and what about the guilt, Kate? I feel relieved and guilty at the same time." Said Delia.

"It's completely normal to feel that, but you shouldn't feel guilty Delia, like I said to Pete 'it takes two'. Did you tell Rob or whatever his name is?"

"No way," Said Delia.

"Well it seems to me, you've had a lucky escape," I said.

Her cramps came on again so Kate gave Delia some painkillers and tucked her up in bed.

"I don't know about you Tess, but it's still too early for me to be up, it's only six o'clock and my head is pounding so I'm back to bed," said Kate.

"Me too," I said, "and by the way Dermott says he will see us tomorrow, what's that about?"

"Tell you later," she said and we both went back to bed.

I wakened a couple of hours later to the smell of coffee.

"I've been up to the farmhouse," said Kate, "Mrs Dieter has sold me eggs, bacon and her homemade bread. We can have a really good breakfast today."

Delia groaned. "Don't talk about breakfast please, I still feel bad."

"You need to take it easy today Delia, I'll get you some more painkillers in a bit, try and sleep for now."

"I couldn't sleep after I went to bed," said Kate," I kept going back to that terrible time with Pete. He was very kind to me but I think that was the first time I realised we wanted different futures. He wanted marriage and settling down. I wanted to live a bit and have some adventures first."

"Well I think your wish has come true this week," I said and laughed.

"Maybe." She smiled, and then changing the subject: "I'm worried about Lizzy, obviously she didn't come home last night. What if she doesn't come back today?"

"Of course she will," I replied, hoping to sound more confident than I felt. "Let's go and see how Ploddy is after her experiences from last night, then we can have some breakfast. I'm sure Lizzy will be back by then."

I linked arms with Kate and we walked slowly to see Ploddy. She didn't seem any the worse for the extra exercise last night. When we gave her an apple she actually seemed pleased to see us, though it could have been the apple.

We stroked her and I murmured a few words of apology in her ear.

After walking for about an hour we made our way back to camp. Delia was up and looking a bit better though still very pale.

"No sign of Lizzy?" asked Kate.

"Not yet, but don't worry about her, she'll be fine," said Delia, "she is good at looking after herself, she has to be."

"What do you mean she has to be?" I asked.

"Her parents are loaded but they just have no time for Lizzy, sent to boarding school from 8 to 18, dished out to various relatives during school holidays, Lizzy has learned to be very self sufficient."

"I didn't know it was as bad as that," said Kate thoughtfully. Having had a couple of conversations with Lizzy I realised that she must be a very unhappy girl. It set me to thinking how lucky I was to have had my own wonderful mother and a family who loved each other. I realised I had a lot to be thankful for.

Just as Delia finished telling us this we heard voices and laughter, one of them Lizzy's. She was walking up the drive, holding hands with the same James she had met last night.

"Would you mind if I went back to bed for a bit?" asked Delia, "I can't face Lizzy just yet."

Unlike us, Lizzy looked full of the joys of spring, in fact she looked happier than she ever had since we met in Dublin those few days ago, although it felt a lot longer.

"Hi, you met James last night do you remember? God, you two look like you had a heavy night."

"I guess you could say that," said Kate.

"And where's Delia?"

"Still sleeping it off I'm afraid," I replied.

"Well I'll try not to disturb her, but I just have to get something from the caravan."

Two minutes later she was back with her sketch pad and handed it to James.

After leafing through a few pages he remarked, "Lizzy these are fab, I would have no problem selling your work. Come back to London with me and I'll sort it all out." Lizzy just smiled.

"Would you like to stay for breakfast or a coffee?" I asked.

"Thanks, a coffee would be good," said James.

"You both seem happy," I said.

"What a week I am having," said Lizzy, "I thought Delia was mad to ask me on this trip and I haven't exactly tried to make the most of it. But if I hadn't come I wouldn't have met you, James." She squeezed his hand.

I couldn't help feeling we were all having an eventful week one way or another.

"Breakfast's ready," said Kate. We sat outside, enjoying the sun as well as the very tasty bacon.

Over breakfast Lizzy and James told us just how lucky they were to find each other. He was here on holiday with his family and had come to Ryans last night to hear the band.

"We spent nearly all night talking," said Lizzy, "and James has offered to help me sell some of my sketches, if they're good enough."

Her plan was to go to London and fund herself through Art College. James had graduated last year and had contacts. She could even stay with his family until she was on her feet. From his response to her sketch pad he clearly thought her drawings were good enough.

"James's parents are lovely, and his sisters. I met them all last night, they have a holiday cottage not that far from here on the coast. This holiday is turning out better than I ever thought it could. In fact it could even change my life." she held James' hands across the table.

Clearly Lizzy and James were smitten, they were practically glowing at each other, eyes ablaze, and suddenly Lizzy stood up: "I can't wait to tell Delia, I think I'll see if she's awake yet."

"No, Lizzy don't do that," said Kate, "she had a bad night."

"I'm sure she won't mind when she hears what I have to tell her."

Lizzy started towards the van.

"I said don't, please don't wake her," said Kate.

"Honestly Kate, I am just too happy to get mad with you but why are you stopping me talking to Delia, she is my friend after all, more of..."

I interrupted her. "You can't leave college now, with just one year to go. You are only nineteen and not legally responsible." It sounded pathetic, but I was thinking of Delia and her not being ready to speak to Lizzy.

"What do you mean, not responsible," said Lizzy, "I am the only one who really cares about me. My parents don't give a damn, they want a goody goody daughter who's happy to be married off to someone they approve of, they already have one or two lined up."

"But Lizzy," I said, "you're two thirds through the course ..."

"Buggar college, and buggar you two. For your information I will be twenty one in six months time, I had to repeat some of my sixth form when my parents realised I was deliberately failing. It didn't work out well, they threatened all sorts so I gave in."

Lizzy was shouting now, "But I'm not giving in this time. They won't even miss me for the next six months because they will be too busy organizing and celebrating my brother's graduation. James has offered me a way out and I'm damn well going to take it."

She stopped yelling when Delia came stumbling out of the caravan.

"Oh God Delia you look awful, what's happened?"

Saying nothing, Delia went to her friend, threw her arms round her neck and began to cry.

"Hey Delia don't cry, you know I won't disappear, you're my friend and always will be." But Delia couldn't stop.

"Listen, Lizzy," I said gently, "Delia isn't crying over you, go inside with her and I'll bring you both a drink."

Then turning to James I suggested he find somewhere to go, perhaps come back in an hour or two.

"That's fine with me," he said, "I'm not very good with all this emotional stuff."

"Ha," replied Kate, "you've seen nothing yet," and she marched off.

James left, promising to be back.

Chapter Ten Thursday afternoon and evening.

When I took the coffee into Lizzy and Delia they were in tears and holding on to each other earnestly. It was clear they were really close friends and I was glad for them. About an hour later I peeped in to see if they wanted another drink. They were fast asleep in each others arms, it had been a momentous night for them both, and I guessed they were exhausted.

I stepped out the door just as James arrived back from his walk.

"Hi, is Lizzy in there? I need to see her."

"She's a bit busy but won't be too long, why don't you sit here and wait for her?"

I pointed to the folding stool we had found in the caravan.

"I'm Tess by the way, it was a bit noisy last night and I didn't talk much to anyone."

Now I could see him in daylight, I could see why Lizzy was attracted to him, not just because he was great looking, with his floppy blonde hair and glasses, there was definitely something more. Maybe the sparkling eyes and the rugby player build, which was impressive.

"Did you mean what you said to Lizzy about going to London?" I asked.

"Yes I did, as Lizzy said we spent most of last night talking, it turns out we have a lot of interests in common, especially art. I can sort of understand why she's so unhappy and I think I can help her."

"Help her to do what exactly?" I said, sounding much more aggressive than I intended. He gave me a look.

"Sorry," I said, "that came out wrong, I'm not a close friend of Lizzy, and Delia is her friend. The only time Kate and I have spent with Lizzy is on this holiday, and even though we don't know her that well, she's told us enough for us to realise she is very unhappy. I'm just looking out for her, wouldn't want her to jump from the frying pan into the fire if you know what I mean."

"I know exactly what you mean," came Lizzy's voice behind me.

"But Tess, you really don't need to worry. James is going to give me the chance I've been waiting for and as I said earlier I'll soon be twenty one and in a better position to make my own choices. If he can really help me sell a few paintings then I am going to re-apply to Art College in London."

"And Tess," added James, "even though I may not have known Lizzy for very long, I know enough for me to realise I would never hurt her in any way." I understood what he meant. Lizzy was beaming at James, I left them to it.

I walked up the track into the next field, half looking for Ploddy horse and Kate, but preoccupied with my own thoughts. Truth is I felt jealous of Lizzy, she was able to step out and start again with her life, and with a possible new boyfriend to boot. While I felt... what did I feel, I knew but was ashamed to admit it, I felt trapped. I was crying again before I even realised it.

"Tess," Lizzy was calling to me, "wait a minute."

She soon caught me up and I desperately tried to hide my tears.

"James has gone to pack, so I wanted to thank you. But hey you're crying too."

"Sorry," I said. It was all I could say.

"Look Tess," said Lizzy, "I know that you are very sad about losing your Mum, and I also know there is nothing I can say that will make you feel better, I really wish there was." She took my hand. "But there is something I do want to say. Thanks for what you said to James about me, it feels good to hear someone looking out for me, and I know Delia feels the same. She told me how great you and Kate were this morning. It must have been awful for all of you."

"I think Delia is the one who really suffered," I said.

Lizzy shook her head. "It's not all bad though, is it Tess?"

"Well it's a bit of a mess right now but I expect she will feel differently when she gets home."

"I agree with you on that."

"What are you going to do Lizzy? Are you really going to London?"

"I'm definitely not going home, but you don't need to worry about me. My parents will create merry hell but they will calm down eventually. I've been threatening to leave home for the last year and now the right opportunity has come along, thanks to you and Kate."

"How do you work that out?"

"Well if Delia hadn't persuaded me to come on this holiday I would not be feeling as happy as I am right now with James. He is travelling home today with his family and will meet me when I get back to London."

She put her arm through mine and walked me back to the caravan.

"Do you know what, Tess, I am feeling so happy I think I'll have a go at making our dinner tonight."

"Well that's a reason to celebrate, and Kate will be delighted." I smiled at her.

Kate was marching towards us.

"Where are you going," I asked.

"To see Ploddy, she's the only one round here I can talk to."

"Hey, guess what, Lizzy is making dinner for us tonight," I said.

"Life is full of surprises," she called back to us as she marched on towards the field. She seemed annoyed about something but I had no idea what. Delia was emerging just as we arrived back. She looked a bit better, certainly not so pale as earlier.

By the time Kate came back the lunch sandwiches were made and we were sitting enjoying the sunshine.

"How is the horse?" I asked.

"Big and white," she replied. Then turning to Delia, "how are you feeling?"

"Much better but still a bit weak," said Delia.

"You will for the rest of the day I should think," said Kate.

As we sat down I asked about Dermott's comment as he had left this morning.

Kate sighed, "Oh that, he offered to fix the tarp for us if I would go for a ride with him. I said I would only go as long as you three came too."

"I vaguely remember that conversation from last night" I said

"I know, and I told him again it was all of us or none. Then he said okay, but only if I sat in the front of the car with him. He's offered to take us for a tour of Connemara."

"I hope you said yes!" said Delia.

"Of course, we've been here almost a week and I would really like to see a bit more of Ireland than a horse's bum, a bog and a few fields. I suppose I could put up with him for an hour or two."

"I thought you liked him," said Delia.

"Well I don't dislike him but I don't want to be going off with him. Anyway I thought it would be nice for all of us to see a bit more than the twenty miles we've come with Ploddy horse."

We laughed.

"I don't know why you're laughing, I'm sacrificing myself for you all." said Kate,

"Hardly a sacrifice! I saw and heard you snogging last night. Don't tell me you don't fancy him," I said.

"I was drunk last night and that's all I'm going to say about it. He's coming this afternoon to fix the tarp and will pick us up at ten tomorrow morning."

She looked at us doubtfully. "You are going to come aren't you?"

"Of course," said Lizzy, "I can't wait to see how you handle him, he really likes you, couldn't take his eyes off you last night."

Kate actually blushed. "Oh shut up," she said. We ignored her discomfort and gave up teasing her after a while.

"Well that's tomorrow sorted, but what are we going to do for the rest of today?" asked Lizzy.

"I'm going to lie down again," said Delia "I'm still feeling a bit wiped out."

"I think I'll just stay here and read my book. It's a nice day and it will make a change to just sit quietly for a while," I said.

"Well I guess I should go shopping since I've said I'll cook dinner tonight. Do you fancy coming with me Kate?" asked Lizzy.

I looked at Kate, Kate looked at Lizzy: "Okay then," she said. "Why not?"

Turning to me she said, "Dermott will be here in an hour or two but we will be back by then." She smiled at me and winked.

It was very pleasant sitting in the calm of the afternoon and I didn't notice Dieter coming down the track from the Farm house.

"Hello there I just come to tell you that I have moved the horse to another field, I have to fix a gate."

"Thanks for letting us know," I said.

"Do you want some supplies tomorrow?"

"Yes thank you, someone will call for them. Did you remember we will be leaving on Saturday morning?"

"That's good." Said Dieter, "Let me know what time and I'll bring the horse down."

"I can tell you tomorrow after I've spoken to the others, I think it will be early."

"Good," he said and walked on.

About an hour later Delia woke so we put on the kettle and we had just settled down with our drinks when Kate and Lizzy arrived back. They seemed to be getting on well for a change.

"What's for dinner then?" I asked.

"Sausages, beans and mash," Lizzy replied. "I'll just go and do a few more drawings for my portfolio, Kate."

"Okay," Kate said without a trace of sarcasm or ill feeling.

I was very relieved, Delia was smiling.

"Before you ask Kate, I am feeling even better than the last time you asked," said Delia.

"I'm glad to hear it" said Kate, "I think I'll just have time for some tea before Dermott arrives to fix the tear, he only has an hour to spare so he won't be here long."

"Do you want Delia and I to disappear for a bit when he arrives?"

"Don't you dare! I mean it Tess, I don't want to be on my own with him, no matter what you heard last night."

"All right, don't get your knickers in a twist Kate, we'll stay won't we Delia?"

Delia was laughing so much she could only nod.

Over her cup of tea Kate told us how well things had gone with Lizzy.

"Once we started listening to each other it was fine. Of course we are from very different backgrounds but we do have some things in common..."

"Look! What's wrong with Lizzy," asked Delia.

We turned to see Lizzy charging down the path towards us. She was out of breath by the time she got to us and could hardly speak.

"It's ... the ... horse."

"Oh my God!" said Kate, "Don't tell me the bloody thing is dead. I know I didn't like her much but I don't want her to die, what happened to her Lizzy?"

"I don't know, she's gone that's all."

Then I remembered Dieter's message. When I told them they set about me with relieved fake punches.

"I wouldn't really have been surprised if she had died," said Kate, "what else can go wrong with this holiday."

"Looks like Dermott's hero," I said and this time we all laughed.

Dermott parked behind the caravan.

"Yous all look happier than the last time I saw you, he said.

"Well that's because we are," said Lizzy. Delia and I just smiled.

"I can only spare an hour, but that should be enough," said Dermott.

Kate went to fetch the repair materials we had bought and Dermott collected a box of tools from the car.

"I don't know if I have something here that'll help, I think it's going to need more brute strength than anything else. Have you got any more of those big safety pins Kate?" said Dermott.

We produced the tape and pins.

"Ah, nappy pins! Just the job," he said with a smile. "Now I'll get my ladder."

He brought a small set of ladders from the boot of the car.

"I made this myself, just right for jobs like this and I can get them in the car easy enough."

"And how many times have you had to repair a tarpaulin on a caravan?" asked Kate.

"Well not that many to be honest but I'll give anything a go," he said, giving Kate a rather obvious wink.

I nudged her. "He's yours for the taking," I whispered in her ear.

Giving me one of her Kate glares she said, "Why don't you get the stool Tess and you can stand on it and help Dermott pull the tarp together."

"Good idea," said Dermott.

We pulled the tarp down and Kate caught the edges together and pinned them using all the safety pins we had. When that was done Dermott applied the tape. Within an hour the job was done and although not perfect, the tarp certainly looked better.

"Have you told the others about our trip out tomorrow?" Dermott asked Kate.

"Oh yes, and we are all really looking forward to it," Kate answered.

"Shame I can't take you out tonight," said Dermott, "but I have to work on the house today if I want a day off tomorrow."

"Yes, it's a pity," said Kate, "but never mind, we'll have a great time tomorrow."

"Oh yes I'm sure we will," said Dermott with another wink at Kate.

He finished clearing up his ladder and tools and we waved him off.

"I guess that's a good example of blarney," I said, but no-one took any notice.

"Shall I start on dinner?" asked Lizzy.

"Good idea," said Kate, "would you like me to peel the potatoes?"

This reformation of Kate was amazing, I just hoped it would last.

With only the lightest of guidance from Kate, Lizzy made us a very good dinner which was even better when she produced the HP sauce.

By the time we had finished the meal and the clearing up it was early evening.

"Any ideas what we can do tonight?" asked Kate.

"Well, I don't want to go anywhere," said Delia.

"Drinks and cards would suit me," I said.

"Me too," said Lizzy.

"Thank goodness for that," said Kate, "it's been a long and eventful day."

I got out the cards while Kate produced the vodka and Lizzy the orange squash.

"Before we start," said Delia, "I would like to say something to you Kate, and you Tess. I don't know how to thank you for what you did for me this morning. When I woke up with the pain I looked for Lizzy but she wasn't there."

"I am so sorry," said Lizzy, taking Delia's hand.

"I know you are Lizzy, but how could you know what was happening to me, luckily I had two other friends who could help, so please don't feel bad about it."

"Even if I had been here," said Lizzy, "I don't know if I could have been as efficient as you two were."

"I wouldn't say that," said Kate, "sometimes we don't know what we are capable of until there is a crisis. I only knew what had happened because of my own experience."

"You mean it's happened to you?" said Lizzy, looking rather surprised.

"Yes it has, and I have a good idea of what you are feeling now Delia, relieved but guilty, am I right?"

Delia nodded, she couldn't speak.

Kate put an arm around her shoulder. "It's a hard lesson Delia but I promise you will be all right."

"Oh I don't know," she said quietly, "I was drunk and then the horse riding, I keep trying to remember what I was thinking, did I do it on purpose? I don't know if I was thinking at all, but that's still wrong isn't it? I should have thought of the baby."

"It's always easy to blame yourself," I said, "but that isn't going to help you now. You're only nineteen and with your life in front of you, you'll have learned from this Delia."

"They're right Delia," said Lizzy, "you didn't want this to happen, but it has, and I am sure it will help you decide what you really want for your future." She hugged her friend.

"What a week this is turning out to be," said Kate.

"And it's not over yet," I added. "Now what are we going to play first, whist, rummy or Newmarket?"

Chapter Eleven- Friday

The next day it was me who was up first. The sun was shining and there was only a breath of wind, it looked as if it was going to be a very good day for our trip. I put the kettle on and pretty soon the others were awake. Delia, feeling better, said she would make the breakfast. Lizzy took the kitty purse and went up to the farmhouse to buy some milk and eggs.

"Don't forget to tell Dieter we're leaving tomorrow," said Kate, "and change the subject if he mentions the gate or ripped canvas."

"Of course," Lizzy replied.

We had our usual light wipe with a flannel and now, after a couple of days without a proper wash, the vapour of spray deodorant filled the caravan. I went outside for some fresh air and Lizzy arrived back.

"Mrs Dieter didn't mention anything," she reported on her return.

"That's good," said Kate. "Now we all need to get a move on, Dermot will be here in about half an hour."

She was right, we were just finishing breakfast when Dermot drove through the gate. He had borrowed his brother's car, a large Vauxhall, very smart.

At the last minute Lizzy tried to get out of the trip.

"I think I'd like to stay here and finish some of my drawings," she said.

"Oh no, don't you know yet, we are All for one and one for All," said Kate.

I gave a half hearted cheer.

Kate continued, "I think we should all be together for our last adventure. The way this holiday is going I wouldn't be surprised at anything that happens today and I certainly don't want you to miss it."

Delia added, "You know you will regret it later Lizzy, and anyway I still need your support so you've got to come." She took Lizzy's arm and dragged her towards the car.

"Okay I give in, let me get my little sketch pad, I might see something worth drawing I suppose," said Lizzy.

"Are we ready?" said Dermot, "Let's get going. Kate you're in the front with me, and there's plenty of room in the back for the rest of you."

He was smiling hopefully at Kate but she wasn't giving much of a response. We all got in the car, ready for our last full day in Ireland.

Just before we set off Dermott turned to Delia.

"How are you feeling now? I thought you still looked a bit rough yesterday."

"I'm fine, thank you Dermot. Obviously Guinness in Ireland is a bit stronger than at home."

Lizzy and I squeezed Delia's hands.

"You're right about that," he said. He turned the key and we were on our way.

"I thought we would go along to Spiddal and see the sea, then up to Maam Cross, down to Oughterard, then home. It's about eighty miles all together."

"That sounds great," said Kate, "I guess we can stop somewhere as well."

"Of course," said Dermot, "we have to call in at the Spiddal ice cream shop, it's famous round here. Then we can stop for some fish and chips on the way home."

We made general noises of approval in the back seat.

"Just one thing," said Dermot, "I have to just call in at the house for a minute, it's on our way so it won't take us off the route."

He was right, it wasn't far to his home but it wasn't quite what we were expecting. Dermott jumped out of the car as soon as we pulled up so we were left to wonder.

"My God," said Lizzy, "does anyone live in a place like that."

She was saying what we were all thinking, it was the kind of place that looked quaint from a distance, white painted farmhouse with thatched roof, but close up we could see the thatch was old and in need of repair. It was single storey with a window to each side of the central front door. The windows were small and it looked dark inside. Dilapidated was the word that came to mind. Next to the house was a sort of barn and a hundred yards from the barn there were building works. It wasn't clear what was being built. True to his word, within minutes Dermott was on his way back to the car.

"Shh..., don't say anything," Kate said.

"Wow," said Lizzy as soon as Dermott was in the car, "that looks like a really old house, have your family lived there long?"

Kate sighed.

"My great grandfather built it and I was born there," said Dermott.

"How many are there in your family?" I asked.

"My Mam had six boys and two girls, most folk round here have big families."

"That must have been a squash," I said.

"No, not really, we had the barn too, so plenty of room for the boys to sleep in there. We did alright, no-one died young so there's six of us now building the new house. My sisters are married and there's me and Eamon left at home with Mam and Dad."

"Is that the new house next door?" asked Kate.

"Yes, we work on it when we can, we want it finished by Christmas. It'll be grand when it's done, proper bathroom and a modern kitchen."

Dermott went on to explain what his family was doing was common practice in most of rural Ireland. It gave us all food for thought.

"Isn't this the road to Moycullen?" asked Lizzy.

"Yes, we drive through," said Dermott.

"Hope you don't need to get any petrol," Kate said.

"You're right to be worried Kate, maybe the Garda are still looking for us for causing criminal damage," I said, with a laugh.

"What are youse talking about?" asked Dermott.

I filled him in with interruptions and additions from the other three.

"Just as well I filled up first then, I didn't know I was driving a bunch of criminals. Damages to a petrol pump, gate and caravan. A right trail of disaster you've made girls."

We laughed but Kate didn't seem to think it was that funny.

Dermott noticed, "Aw come on," he said, "it was only a joke, can ye not take a joke?"

Kate looked round at us, she didn't look happy.

"Kate, you have to admit it is funny looking back at it even if it wasn't at the time," I said, but she said nothing then turned back, shuffling towards the door as she did so.

Dermott was talking softly to Kate so we three chatted between ourselves, mostly about how long it had taken to walk this road with Ploddy compared to the speed we were now travelling.

"Heads down girls, petrol station coming up," said Dermott.

"He hasn't fixed the pump yet," said Lizzy, "probably waiting for the next one who hits it to pay," she said, laughing.

We were passing the Moycullen bogs and Dermott told us a little bit of the history and uses of the peat bog.

"We still use it as fuel even today. Hey, but wait a minute, isn't that the place we first met Kate?"

He slowed down as we passed the infamous lay by of our humiliation. He was right, I could feel myself blushing and couldn't bear to look at Kate.

"Look at the wall," said Delia, "it's still standing."

"We made a good job of that," said Lizzy.

Kate and I said nothing. I could see Dermott's face in the mirror, he was smiling broadly.

"Not far to Spiddal now, we can stretch our legs and see the sea," he said.

"Isn't this the road we have to travel tomorrow?" I asked.

"Aye," replied Dermott.

"How far is it to Barna from where the caravan is now?" asked Kate.

"Oh I'd say around ten."

"What! We've only done about twenty miles in the whole week. Can we do ten miles in a day? We have to be back there by four to get the bus to Dublin," said Kate.

We all knew what Kate meant, it was impossible to imagine Ploddy horse getting us there in time.

"Don't worry Kate, we'll leave early and we'll beat the ploddy horse to go faster if we have to," said Lizzy.

Kate looked shocked.

"I'm joking," said Lizzy.

But I wasn't so sure, I was worried Ploddy wouldn't go any faster than her normal slow plod. Still I didn't want to beat her.

"Remember the other night?" said Dermott, "she went fast enough then, and once she knows she is going home, she'll pick up speed." I was a bit sceptical about that.

"Oh we remember the other night all right," said Delia, "but I would much rather forget it." Another hand squeeze for Delia from Lizzy and I.

We turned on to the coast road and I, at least, immediately felt better for seeing the sea.

"Here we are girls, lovely Spiddal with a great view of Galway Bay." announced Dermott

He parked near the beach, we piled out of the car and Lizzy organised us.

"Here Delia, link your arm through mine and your other one with Tess, we'll look after you," said Lizzy winking at Kate.

"The ice cream place is just along the beach by the pier," said Dermott.

He was making an attempt to hold Kate's hand but she brushed him off.

It was actually more of a harbour sea wall, than a pier, some bobbing fishing boats and a brisk wind. There were a few families on the beach, paddling and enjoying picnics. The ice-cream shop was busy and there was a queue.

"Should we wait for the love-birds," said Delia.

"I don't know about that, look at them," I said.

They were about fifty yards away walking very slowly towards us, and they were not close together. As we watched they stopped, Kate facing Dermott, she took his hands and there was some earnest talk on her part. Dermott did not seem to be saying much. Then she kissed him and, still holding his hand, walked towards us smiling.

"What's going on there, this morning she could hardly bear to look at him, now she's kissing him!" said Lizzy.

"That's true, but Dermott doesn't look too happy," said Delia.

I had to agree, but I would have to get Kate on her own to find out what was going on.

"I guess we'll find out soon enough, but one thing's for sure, whatever Kate wants, Dermott won't stand a chance against her," I said.

"No, she'll make mincemeat out of him right enough," said Delia.

As they came closer we could see Kate seemed a lot happier than she had been an hour ago, Dermott just looked baffled.

"You were right about the ice-cream Dermott, it's fantastic," said Lizzy.

"I knew you'd like it, I'll go and get us some Kate," he said.

As soon as he was out of earshot I asked Kate what had happened.

"What are you talking about?" she said. "Nothing has happened, I just put him straight about a few things that's all, we're still friends."

She would not be drawn any further. We could see Dermott on his way back.

"I know there is more to it," I whispered to Kate.

"Tell you later," she replied and smiling sweetly she took the proffered ice-cream from Dermott.

We made our way back to the car, Kate and Dermott out in front. Kate was happy but poor Dermott still looked confused.

"We just do a few more miles along the coast and then turn towards Oughterard," said Dermott.

"Isn't that the place with the donkey?" I asked.

"Yes, I remember it well, it's where Kate and I had a big fallout," said Lizzy.

"That's right," said Kate," it seems a long time ago, before I knew you Lizzy."

"And now that you know me better, what do you think," said Lizzy.

"I'd say you're okay for a Southerner," Kate said with a laugh.

"I'll take that as a sort of compliment," replied Lizzy with a smile.

"Do any of yous know a film called 'The Quiet Man'?" asked Dermott.

"It was one of my Mum's favourites," I replied. "She loved John Wayne." For a moment I smiled. "Wasn't it set around this part of Ireland?"

"Not just set, it was filmed here and we're going to see the bridge where there was a famous scene, it's near Boffin Lake."

"Great," said Lizzy.

I wasn't sure if she was being sarcastic or not. We chatted on with Kate turning and joining in with us, completely ignoring Dermott. I was beginning to feel a bit sorry for him.

"I can't believe we have only been away from home for a week," I said.

"I know what you mean," said Kate, "feels more like a month to me."

"More like a lifetime for me," said Delia with a faraway look.

"And for me," concluded Lizzy.

"Here we are," said Dermott pulling of the road. "This is the famous bridge that was in the film, The Quiet Man. John Wayne sat here looking across the valley to the house where he was born, in the film of course."

We had got out of the car to take a photo of the bridge, it was pretty rather than impressive. Stone built with, unusually, two arches. We walked back and forth, looking at the river that was actually not much more than a stream, running below us. It began to drizzle or soft rain as the Irish called it.

"Time to go," said Dermott. As we walked towards the car he swore loudly.

"Jesus Christ I don't believe it, a bloody puncture."

He was right, the front nearside tyre was as flat as a pancake.

"Is there a spare?" asked Kate.

"Yes and a jack, but I could do without this. Eamon will blame me for it."

He pulled the spare, jack and wheel wrench out of the boot and began the process of removing and replacing the wheel.

"I'll need to get some air in this spare before we go much further," he said.

"Is there anything we can do?" I asked.

"No you're fine, I've done this plenty of times."

When he dropped the car down and removed the jack it was obvious the tyre needed some air.

"Here Kate take the jack and put it in the boot, I'll just tighten the nuts," said Dermott.

It was a scissor jack and a bit awkward to hold although not that heavy, Kate picked it up and carried it to the boot. She was just about to put it in when Dermott came up behind her. He put his arm round her waist as he threw in the wheel wrench. Kate, caught by surprise, turned round and promptly dropped the jack on his foot.

"Jesus, Mary and Joseph," he shouted as he hopped about, then his language got a lot worse.

"God Dermott, I'm so sorry, how bad is it?" asked Kate.

"Bad enough," he yelled at her.

He was wearing plimsolls which didn't offer much protection from falling jacks and he had now pulled his plimsoll off the affected left foot.

"Is it bleeding?" said Kate

"No, but it's swelling and it bloody hurts."

"What are we going to do?"

"Yous'll have to get the wheel in the car, we'll get some air in the tyre at Oughterard and go home."

"But you might have broken a bone or something..." started Kate.

"Ye mean YOU might have broken a bone or something."

Dermott glared at her and hopped round to the front of the car.

Lizzy and I helped Kate get the wheel into the boot.

Dermott said nothing more, but got into the car and we followed him.

The next fifteen minutes was filled with his swearing in pain. We carried on with us sitting there in awkward silence. I don't know how he managed to drive if he was in so much agony. At last a garage came into view.

"Do any of you know how to put air in a tyre?" asked Dermott.

"I do," replied Lizzy. "What pressure?" she asked.

"Till it's hard," was Dermott's reply.

When she had finished she opened Dermott's door.

"I know you won't like what I'm about to say, Dermott, but you know you can't drive safely any further. So change seats with Kate and I'll take over."

"No, no I can manage."

"You clearly can't, and don't worry I took my test a couple of months ago."

Delia and I looked at each other.

"But this is a big car and it's my brother's," he said a bit sheepishly. "He'll kill me if I damage it."

"You haven't and I won't, my dad has a big car so I'm used to them."

"Are you really sure?"

Lizzy assured him she was, and that she could drive, once she knew where the gears were. She gave the three of us a swift and sharp warning look.

"Say nothing," whispered Delia.

I was too surprised to say anything and Kate just looked astonished.

"Okay then, but mind and listen to what I'm telling you," said Dermott.

Lizzy adjusted the seat and sat behind the wheel. She must have caught sight of Delia's alarmed face as she turned to reverse. We said nothing. There was a bit of gear crunching, but at least she seemed to know what she was doing and once we were in top gear her steering improved. Dermott was so anxious he almost forgot about his foot but once or twice I heard him swear under his breath. No-one spoke for the whole journey, we were all on tenterhooks. Turning right was traumatic for us all but Lizzy did okay and after about an hour at a top speed of 30mph, we approached the farmhouse.

Dermott grudgingly thanked Lizzy and ignoring the rest of us completely, opened the door to get out of the car. Unfortunately Eamon, his brother, and the car owner, was standing outside the house as we drew up, so he knew straight away something was wrong.

He came marching over as Dermott struggled out.

"Don't worry," said Dermott, "as long as the car is okay he'll be fine."

As they were having their heated exchange we got out of the car.

By this time Mam had arrived on the scene, asked what happened and then instructed Dermott to show her his foot.

"You'll need an X-ray for that, Eamon'll take you to the hospital once he's taken the girls to wherever they're going."

She gave us a look which clearly said, "Away from here you floozies!"

I thought Kate might have something to say, but she just muttered another apology and got back in the car with the rest of us. We waited for Eamon.

"Don't you want to say goodbye to Dermott properly Kate? You might not see him again," said Delia.

"Don't worry about me," she said as Eamon got in beside her.

"What happened to his foot?" Eamon asked as soon as he was seated.

Kate went in to a long rambling account of our trip with Dermott and what had happened to his foot. It was clear she was spinning out the yarn for as long as possible, giving him little chance to ask awkward questions like, "Why was he taking you all out in my car in the first place?"

Kate's ploy worked and we arrived back at the caravan just as she had related how lucky it was Lizzy could drive his lovely car, and we all arrived safely home. He was muttering under his breath as we got out and started revving up before the last door was shut. We stood and watched him drive out of the farm, on to the road and away from us forever. Then all four of us laughed and laughed, in fact too busy laughing to notice Dieter coming down from the farm.

Chapter Twelve - Friday Evening

"Hallo girls, what time are you going tomorrow? I will bring the horse down for you."

"Oh hello Dieter, that's very kind of you, we need to leave really early," I said.

"I can come down about six, is that okay?"

I must have looked shocked.

"We had thought about eight that will be early enough." We had worked out that if we left about eight a.m. with Ploddy covering two miles per hour, walking pace, even with a short break we should be back in Barna in plenty of time.

The other three nodded in approval.

"Eight o'clock then," said Dieter, "I will see you then."

He turned and made his way back up to the farmhouse.

"Did you see his face?" said Delia.

"I didn't notice, but I don't expect he was crying," said Kate.

"Not sure if it was a smirk or a smile, but I think he will be happy to see us leave," said Delia.

"No surprise there. What shall we do now?" I asked, "Seeing that Dermott's accident has left us stranded."

"I'm hungry, can we go and eat, anything would be good," said Delia, "I don't think I've eaten anything at all today."

"Shame about missing out on Connemara," said Lizzy, "but even more shame to miss out on fish and chips."

"Let's go then, we'll get a lift or bus to Salthill, Dermott said there's some good fish shops there," said Kate.

"Ohhh Dermott says..." said Lizzy.

"Shut up Lizzy or I might just drop something on your foot, not that I dropped that jack on purpose."

I had witnessed the incident so jumped in to defend my friend.

"Of course you didn't, but you must admit it was convenient, if you didn't like him I mean."

Three of us were looking at Kate expectantly but she wasn't in the mood for explaining anything.

"Come on, let's finish off the kitty," she said.

We waited at the bus stop but we had decided if we saw any large cars coming our way we would hitch a lift. We had only been there about five minutes when a large and shiny Rover appeared so we stuck out our thumbs and the car slowed. As it neared us, I realised too late it was a priest driving.

"Hello Father," Kate said as he wound down the window, "are you going into Galway?"

"Why yes I am, in you get plenty of room in this car."

Kate was determined this time not to be in the front, even with a priest, and she pushed me forwards to the front door while she and the others climbed into the back.

"I'm Father Michael Ryan and what are your names?"

We introduced ourselves though Lizzy, being Lizzy, introduced herself as Marilyn.

"Have you been for a walk?"

"Yes," said Lizzy, "we are staying at my auntie's in Salthill and we went for a walk but Kate twisted her ankle and we couldn't go on or walk back so we were hoping someone kind would give us a lift."

I picked up. "Yes it's lucky for us you came along, poor Kate is in agony."

Kate did her best to look as if she was in some kind of agony. We were being careful not to make eye contact, especially when Father Michael suggested Kate should go to the hospital to have it examined. Kate nearly choked.

"No, nothing broken Father," said Delia, "just a bad sprain. I'm training to be a nurse and I am fairly sure Li...Marilyn's auntie will be able to make a compress for her."

"Yes," said Lizzy, "Auntie Gertie will soon sort Kate out. I think you might need something for that cough as well Kate."

And so the banter went on, each trying to top the other with a believable fantasy. The game finished when someone laughed or when the poor person we were lying to eventually twigged. Father Michael was far too trusting and swallowed every word. The game finished when Lizzy (Marilyn) told Father Michael we were entering the convent soon and had been advised to go and get some experience of life.

"Well you could do worse than have a holiday in Galway," said Father Michael, "have you been to our New Cathedral, named after Our Lady Assumed into Heaven and St. Nicholas. It was consecrated just last year. What a grand day that was, Cardinal Cushing led the ceremony you know."

We had seen the Cathedral when we went on the bus into Galway. I was not too impressed, it's a severe looking building but I guess it will mellow over the next hundred or so years.

"I could show you round if you have time girls," said Father Michael.

"That's really kind of you but this is our last day, maybe the next time we're here," said Kate.

"What order are you joining?" Father Michael suddenly asked.

"The Poor Sisters of Mercy" replied Lizzy.

"I don't think I've heard of them," said Father Michael "The Sisters of Mercy were founded in Ireland. Where was your convent founded?"

"Actually" said Lizzy, "not that far from here."

Kate was on the floor behind me trying so hard not to laugh she started snorting.

Father Michael was alarmed, "Is your friend all right, sounds like she is having breathing problems."

"She'll be all right, she has asthma. Actually Father, if you could let us out here we can walk the rest of the way and Kate can get some fresh air," said Lizzy.

"Well if you're sure."

"Oh, yes Father, and thank you so much, I'll tell Auntie Gertie how kind you have been," said Lizzy as we got out of the car.

"Don't forget to limp," she said to Kate under her breath.

Kate nodded, and limped convincingly until the car was out of sight.

"Oh God," said Kate, "what a laugh, though trying not to, nearly choked me."

We re-lived the whole conversation with Father Michael as we made our way to Salthill, but this time letting the laughter rip, it felt so good.

Eventually we quietened down and I fell behind with Kate and took the opportunity of quizzing her about Dermott.

"Okay I'll tell you. I was so drunk on Friday night things went a bit further than they should have, you know what I mean?" I nodded.

"I obviously gave Dermott the wrong impression, I mean he is a nice guy but I made a mistake and realised it well enough. When he started trying to touch me up in the car yesterday I had to tell him."

"Do you mean you didn't fancy him at all?" I asked.

"No, not really, I guess I was just taking advantage of the situation, like we all were. After all, that's what holidays are for isn't it? But I did learn something really important from Dermott. When we reached Spiddal and he started fumbling for my hand. I knew I had to explain myself, I told him that the only person I had kissed before was Pete, my boyfriend from school. As I said it I realised I wasn't feeling guilty about Pete, not in the slightest. What I did want was more kisses from different men. Poor Dermott, he looked so confused so I gave him a big kiss and thanked him for opening my eyes. I absolutely know now I have to finish with Pete, he's not the one for me."

"And how do you feel about that now?"

Kate paused for a bit then replied, "Truthfully Tess, I have a sense of freedom, and it feels just great."

"I'm happy for you Kate, I think you've made the right decision," I said.

"Thanks Tess, now let's catch up with the others and find a fish shop."

We had our last fish and chips of the holiday sitting watching the tide come in at Salthill. It was a glorious evening, probably the best of the holiday. Of course Lizzy and Delia were curious about the Kate and Dermott situation.

"So what's going on or not going on between you and Dermott?" Lizzy asked.

Kate gave her a shortened version of the story she had told me.

"Poor Dermott, I think I led him on a bit, although I didn't mean to. I've been with Pete for so long I'm not really sure how to behave sometimes. I think it's over between us, a twenty four hour romance that's all," said Kate.

Delia was looking really tired so I was very happy to hear Lizzy say: "Let's get a bottle of something and go home to Ploddy horse. There's just enough money to buy some wine, what about 'Blue Nun'?"

"Great idea, very appropriate," said Kate.

Lizzy went to buy some wine while Kate and I linked arms with Delia and started walking towards the main road. As soon as Lizzy joined us we started hitching and unbelievably an army lorry pulled up with a load of squaddies in the back.

"Come on girls jump up," one of them shouted. "How far are you going?"

"Just a couple of miles," I answered.

They helped us up and made room for us.

"Are you British Army, what are you doing in this part of the world?" I asked.

"No, not British, we're the Irish Army, don't tell me you've never heard of us," said one of the soldiers. "We're on our way to training for deployment in Cyprus"

They looked very young for soldiers, although probably about our age.

"The Brits are up North" added one of the soldiers,

"You mean Northern Ireland?"

"Maybe."

"Delia, you have relations in Belfast don't you?" said Lizzy.

Delia was glaring at her and shaking her head.

"Sorry my mistake," Lizzy said. She was looking a bit nonplussed.

"What are you doing here? Obviously not Irish, so guess you must be on holiday?" asked one of the soldiers.

We told them a little about our holiday. I was concerned about Delia, she was looking very pale.

"Are you okay Delia?" I asked, "Are you feeling sick again?"

She nodded. Fortunately we were approaching the field so I asked them to stop. The driver got the message and the lorry pulled to a halt.

We jumped out and shouted our thanks. Delia was still glaring at Lizzy.

"What have I said?" Lizzy asked.

"My grandparents live in Andersonstown and if they knew I had just had a lift with the Army they would not be happy. Thank God it wasn't the British Army, that's all," said Delia.

"But why?" Kate asked.

"Kate I am too tired to talk about it. Let's have the wine and an early night for a change. It's been a long day."

Delia looked exhausted, and I was pretty tired too.

"I'll go and see the horse," said Lizzy.
"And I'll get the glasses," said Kate.

Chapter Thirteen Departures

The noise of the kettle boiling woke me, and I was surprised to see Lizzy was the first one up.

"Morning Tess, just making a coffee for us all. Do you take milk and sugar? How do the others like theirs?"

I gave her the details then commented, "You seem to be in a good mood Lizzy."

"Well can't deny it, I'm going to see James today and I can hardly wait."

I looked at my watch.

"Lord, look at the time, Dieter is going to be here in half an hour. Wake up, you two, and better move fast if you want some breakfast."

There were the usual moans and groans of those not used to rising this early.

"Why the rush? We can tidy things up when we get back to Barna," said Delia.

"That's true," I replied, "but Dieter is bringing Ploddy horse in about twenty minutes, and we have to be ready to harness up. It seems ages since we last had to do it, I hope we can remember."

We managed to bolt down some cereal washed down with coffee before we saw Dieter walking down towards us leading the horse. As he came closer we could see he was smiling. None of us had washed and we were just about dressed but as far as I was concerned the sooner we moved the better. Guilt over the lies we had told him left me feeling very uncomfortable every time I looked at him.

"We'll have to find somewhere on the way for a wash and tidy up but let's get out of here," said Lizzy sounding as keen as I was to get going.

Dieter expertly sorted out the head collar, the bit, the collar, and reins. Kate's pride took over.

"Thank you Dieter, but we can manage the rest," and she went into teacher mode. "Tess can you make sure we have left nothing outside, Delia can you make sure everything is stowed away inside and Lizzy, you help me to get the Bl... Blessed horse into the shafts."

Within fifteen minutes we were ready.

"Thank you for everything Dieter, it's been great staying on your farm," I said.

He nodded in reply, "Your horse has had a good rest, she will move faster. I will just watch as you go through the gates, wouldn't want to have an accident would we."

I didn't know about the others but I just kept my eyes down and said nothing.

This was a challenge, Lizzy and I stood on each side of the horse's head, Kate took up the reins and Delia walked in front ready to stop traffic if we needed to. Kate clicked and flicked the reins and Lizzy and I started the walk down the drive, no-one spoke. Dieter stood at the gate.

"Good-bye Dieter and thanks again," said Kate in a calm voice.

Lizzy and I walked Ploddy horse on, and then turned right, into the traffic free road. There was a bit of a clatter from inside the caravan but we ignored it. I turned round to Kate and caught sight of Dieter shaking his head as he walked away from the road.

Lizzy and I shared our relief that the manoeuvre had gone smoothly. Whatever had clattered seemed to be okay now so nothing was said.

"I'll go back and speak to Kate, find out how she's organising us," Lizzy said with a laugh.

I could hear much discussion going on behind me, though thankfully no raised voices. Ten minutes later Lizzy was back with the plan.

"We'll take it in turn to sort out our stuff, one at a time in the caravan. I am going to take over from you with Ploddy horse so I'm going to walk with you now to see what's what."

"Good plan," I said, "but there's really not that much to walking the horse, just hold her head collar if you see something coming, or any other distraction." This was the last day and the first time Lizzy would be on her own with Ploddy

We changed sides so that Lizzy would get used to being in the middle of the road. She didn't seem at all worried.

"Actually it's quite reviving walking the beast. It's peaceful, and there's time to think," said Lizzy.

"Exactly why I like it," I replied. We walked in silence for a bit. Then Kate called and told me it was my turn in the caravan.

"What was that clattering noise earlier on?" I asked her.

"Delia had a good look round but couldn't see anything, probably the dirty dishes in the bowl."

Delia had stripped her bed and packed her bag, I set about doing the same. It wasn't that easy as the caravan rocked from side to side. When I finished I changed places with Delia on the side seat while she took the reins. Kate swapped places with Lizzy who then started her packing.

"Are you glad you came?" I asked Delia.

"Well, yes, I guess I am, especially as what happened, happened if you know what I mean. I have had time to think as well. One thing I have decided is that I will probably never have sex again. It really wasn't that great anyway and just look what happened as a result."

I laughed. "You'll think differently when you meet someone you really love. At least that's what I'm hoping for, and don't forget we will be able to get the pill soon."

"Do you really think the Church will approve?"

"Yes, not just me saying that. Father Tinnion, the college Chaplin, is saying it's almost certain to be approved. The results of the conference will be published soon."

"Well I'll believe it when it happens. Don't forget the Church is run completely by men, do you really think they worry about the problems women have because of unwanted pregnancies, because I don't."

Lizzy joined in the discussion from behind us.

"You can get the pill now you know, just go to the Family Planning Clinic."

"Don't you have to be married or at least engaged? I thought you had to go as a couple," said Delia.

"Rubbish, just get a ring that looks like an engagement ring and explain that your fiancé works shifts so can't get to the clinic."

"Is that the ring you were wearing when you were travelling to Barna?" I asked.

"I always wear an engagement ring when I'm travelling," said Lizzy, "sometimes a wedding ring if I am on my own and don't want attention."

"How do you know about the Family Planning Clinic?" I asked.

"How do you think?" she said

"Well, you could get away with that Lizzy," said Delia.

"You have the wrong impression of me you know, I was in no hurry to be attached to anyone until I met James, but having been left to my own devices for long periods I know what goes on. It's amazing what you can pick up from conversations on the bus or tube. It's a great way of passing time when home is unbearable," said Lizzy.

There was no answer to that so Delia changed the subject.

"By the way Lizzy, what about that whopping lie you told yesterday about the driving test, which, I happen to know you failed," said Delia.

"I was very careful," said Lizzy "I didn't lie, I said I had taken my test, which is true and that I had driven my father's car which is also true. Anyway Dermott was distracted with the pain and I managed to drive the thing didn't I?"

"You're forgiven Lizzy, don't know what we would have done if you hadn't taken over," I said.

"Your turn Kate," I called.

"I'd like to walk with the Ploddy horse if you don't mind Tess," said Delia.

"Of course, we can change over after lunch," I replied, knowing that, like me, Delia found walking with Daisy was therapeutic.

After the various swaps we carried on steadily for a while. I could hear Delia singing softly to Ploddy horse but despite requests she would not sing up for us.

We were nearing Moycullen and Lizzy offered to go and get something for lunch. As it was a Sunday there would not be a great choice but Kate sent her on her way.

"You go to the shop Lizzy and we will drive on through and meet you at the other end of the town. If anyone asks if you are with those heathens in the caravan, you have my permission to deny any knowledge of us."

"I'm going to miss your sense of humour Kate, when we have to part. Don't let Ploddy horse pull anything down," said Lizzy and she laughed.

"What a difference a week makes," I said, "this time last week you could hardly look at Lizzy, never mind speak to her, and now you're acting like bosom pals."

"You can get used to anything if you try hard enough, as my mother used to say," Kate said.

We pulled in at the first lay-by we came to, rinsed out the cups and put on the kettle. Lizzy was not far behind us with bread, ham, tomatoes and even some cheese. We made our own sandwiches and as soon as we had finished them and our coffee we were on our way.

"Poor horse," I said, "didn't get a chance to stretch her legs on this lunch break."

Time was of the essence and we had left Daisy in the shafts while we had lunch. We had given her a couple of apples in recompense. So far we hadn't found anywhere to wash, but as we were making good time we agreed to press on and get washed when we arrived in Barna.

Lizzy and Delia walked with the horse which left Kate and I in the caravan. I took up the reins and asked Kate the same question I had asked Delia. Was she glad she came?

"Well you know Tess, the first couple of days were really tough and I truly thought I had made a huge mistake, but now we're near the end of the adventure, I have to admit that this holiday has probably changed my life."

"How come?"

"When I left home, last week, I promised Pete I would seriously think about his proposal. Well you know how I feel about that, I love him but didn't want to marry him. When Dermott kissed me I realised my problem. I'm not ready to marry Pete or anyone for that matter. I know Pete wants us to settle down and have a family while we are both young. I don't, I want to see the world and kiss more Dermotts. I do want Pete to be happy but we want different things in life. There are plenty of girls who do want what he wants and he will be much happier with one of them."

"Are you really going to finish with him?"

"As soon as I get home."

"That's going to be hard after all these years."

"It will, but I know it's the right thing to do, we'll both survive."

That word 'survive' really made me think.

"You're very quiet," said Kate.

"I was just thinking if I am glad I came. It's funny you've used the word survive because that's exactly how I felt after the first couple of days. I kept telling myself all I had to do was survive and I would soon be home but the truth is, I'm glad I came but for different reasons from the rest of you. The three of you have all had experiences that have changed you, and now you are excited about moving on with your life, I had my life changing experience six months ago. I wasn't excited about moving on, I miss my Mum too much for that. But this week I have seen it's true what people say, that life goes on anyway. Sometimes it's been fun and sometimes not but I wouldn't have missed it for anything."

"Hey what are you doing back there?" Lizzy shouted just as the horse began to speed up.

"Nothing different, honestly," Kate answered, "can you keep up or do you want me to try and slow her down."

"Well we can still keep up with her at a fast walk pace, but maybe if we take it in turns it won't be too bad. I'll come up with you for ten minutes then I'll swap with Delia."

"That's good because I don't really know how to slow her down, we've never had to do it before."

Lizzy got up onto the seat.

"I think the bloody Ploddy horse knows she's going home, she knows the way," said Lizzy.

Kate began singing 'Three wheels on my wagon' and for the next half hour we swapped places and sang a variety of songs, quite a few of them Irish. Maybe it was the singing, or Ploddy did know her way home, whatever the reason, her pace was steady and definitely up a gear. Dieter had been right about her having more energy.

The horse slowed down as we reached the final road junction and she prepared to turn left. She definitely knew she was going home and the next hour passed really quickly as we changed places every ten minutes. The starting point came into view, we had made good time.

"Buggar," said Kate, "we haven't decided on our story about the rip."

"Don't worry," said Lizzy, "I'll deal with it." She was oozing confidence.

We entered the yard and practically everyone stopped what they were doing when they saw the state of our caravan with its silver stripe. As she had promised Lizzy gave an account to Mr McKeon (call me Frank), on what had happened to the caravan. Her story was based on the one we had given to Dieter, with a few more embellishments, such as reporting the incident to the Garda, who promised they would be in touch with Mr McKeown when they found the offending vehicle with the made up registration.

"By the way," I said "Plo.., I mean Daisy threw a shoe and we had to have a new one, here's the bill that we paid."

Frank scrutinised the receipt before grudgingly pulling some money out of his pocket and paying us.

"Don't worry about the cost of repairs to the caravan I'll give you an address and you can send the bill to my father, he'll pay," finished Lizzy.

Frank didn't look too sure.

"Will he?" I asked when we had moved away from Frank and the van.

"Yes of course, I'll make certain of it. It can be a parting gift to me, though he doesn't know it yet," said Lizzy.

Now we were finished our holiday, I actually felt sad at saying good bye to Ploddy horse. I gave her an affectionate pat, as did the others, but I think I was the only one genuinely sorry to see her leave the yard. She had been a friend when I had been in need.

We were not the last ones in and so there was time for us to have a wash and then to give the caravan a last clean and tidy up. We washed up, wiped down, emptied rubbish and took the bedding to the office as directed. Frank said he would be inspecting all the vans.

The last one trotted into the yard and Frank was not pleased.

"Look at the state of your horse," he said accusingly to the young men

"How far have you travelled today?"

"No further than any other day, about 15 miles."

We looked at each other.

"You've overworked that horse, I gave you the best I had and you've flogged him, don't ever come back here."

Then looking at us he said, "They've done more than fifteen today. I know my beasts."

"Well we certainly didn't flog the..., our horse," I said.

"I can tell that," he replied with a small smile, "but you flogged the van all right."

I cast my eyes down in shame but was thinking it was better than flogging Ploddy horse.

Frank had arranged for some sandwiches while we waited for the bus taking us back to Dublin. While we ate we listened to the other caravaners, tales of meeting friendly people and wonderful views. We didn't say much. Just as we were finishing Frank called to us from our now ex-caravan.

"Did you have a good holiday girls?"

He had a definite leer about him. I was pretty sure he would have received news of our exploits since we had travelled hardly any distance.

"Yes, great thanks," we said almost in unison.

"It looks like it," he smirked and whisked a cover off a box behind him.

It was full of bottles, beer, wine, whisky, vodka and a couple of lemonade.

I looked at the others and guessed we were all thinking the same. Buggar, we had stored ours and the lads' empties in the storage space under the seats. That's what the rattling noise had been.

"Have you anything to say?"

I looked at Lizzy.

"All right, we forgot to remove them but there is a good reason why they are there."

"Go on."

"We are all novices about to enter the convent and were instructed to go out and see a bit of the world before we go any further with preparing our vows. So this last week that's what we have done."

"And where is this convent?" He was definitely smirking.

"Newcastle-on-Tyne, you can ring them if you want but they don't answer the phone except between six pm to nine pm and never on Sundays. Ask for Mother Gaffney," said Kate.

Since it was Sunday we were in the clear, assuming of course that Frank believed us which I very much doubted. He didn't ask for the phone number anyway. We moved the cans and bottles to the bin and then moved ourselves as far as possible from Frank. The bus arrived and we climbed aboard, within fifteen minutes we started the next part of our journey home. An hour later Galway was far behind us. Although we had only been away for a week I was pretty sure our experiences and lessons learned would be with us for a lifetime.

Galway and the Ploddy horse would never be forgotten.

Printed in Great Britain
by Amazon

45123536R00092